"Warrick?"

There was something in C.J.'s voice that made the hair on the back of his neck rise up. He swung around to look at her. She was still sitting at her desk, but there was an odd expression on her face.

"What?"

"How close would you say we were?"

"Pretty close, I guess." Warrick looked at her more intently. "Why?"

C.J. caught her lower lip between her teeth for a second before answering. "I think we're about to get a lot closer."

Like a man feeling his way along a tightrope, Warrick slowly made his way back into the room, staring at C.J. as he came. "What are you talking about?"

"I'm in labor."

Warrick's eyes widened in disbelief, because C.J. was given to practical jokes. "The hell you're not."

C.J. caught her breath, trying to keep her voice steady. "The hell I am."

Dear Reader,

Our exciting month of May begins with another of bestselling author and reader favorite Fiona Brand's Australian Alpha heroes. In *Gabriel West: Still the One*, we learn that former agent Gabriel West and his ex-wife have spent their years apart wishing they were back together again. And their wish is about to come true, but only because Tyler needs protection from whoever is trying to kill her—and Gabriel is just the man for the job.

Marie Ferrarella's crossline continuity, THE MOM SQUAD, continues, and this month it's Intimate Moments' turn. In *The Baby Mission*, a pregnant special agent and her partner develop an interest in each other that extends beyond police matters. Kylie Brant goes on with THE TREMAINE TRADITION with *Entrapment*, in which wickedly handsome Sam Tremaine needs the heroine to use the less-than-savory parts of her past to help him capture an international criminal. Marilyn Tracy offers another story set on her Rancho Milagro, or Ranch of Miracles, with *At Close Range*, featuring a man scarred—inside and out—and the lovely rancher who can help heal him. And in Vickie Taylor's *The Last Honorable Man*, a mother-to-be seeks protection from the man she'd been taught to view as the enemy—and finds a brand-new life for herself and her child in the process. In addition, Brenda Harlan makes her debut with *McIver's Mission*, in which a beautiful attorney who's spent her life protecting families now finds that *she* is in danger—and the handsome man who's designated himself as her guardian poses the greatest threat of all.

Enjoy! And be sure to come back next month for more of the best romantic reading around, right here in Intimate Moments.

Leslie J. Wainger
Executive Senior Editor

Please address questions and book requests to:
Silhouette Reader Service
U.S.: 3010 Walden Ave., P.O. Box 1325, Buffalo, NY 14269
Canadian: P.O. Box 609, Fort Erie, Ont. L2A 5X3

The Baby Mission
MARIE FERRARELLA

INTIMATE MOMENTS™

Published by Silhouette Books

America's Publisher of Contemporary Romance

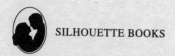 **SILHOUETTE BOOKS**

ISBN 0-373-27290-1

THE BABY MISSION

Copyright © 2003 by Marie Rydzynski-Ferrarella

Books by Marie Ferrarella in Miniseries

ChildFinders, Inc.
A Hero for All Seasons IM #932
A Forever Kind of Hero IM #943
Hero in the Nick of Time IM #956
Hero for Hire IM #1042
An Uncommon Hero Silhouette Books
A Hero in Her Eyes IM #1059
Heart of a Hero IM #1105

Baby's Choice
Caution: Baby Ahead SR #1007
Mother on the Wing SR #1026
Baby Times Two SR #1037

The Baby of the Month Club
Baby's First Christmas SE #997
Happy New Year—Baby! IM #686
The 7lb., 2oz. Valentine Yours Truly
Husband: Optional SD #988
Do You Take This Child? SR #1145
Detective Dad World's Most
   Eligible Bachelors
The Once and Future Father IM #1017
In the Family Way Silhouette Books
Baby Talk Silhouette Books
An Abundance of Babies SE #1422

Like Mother, Like Daughter
One Plus One Makes Marriage SR #1328
Never Too Late for Love SR #1351

The Bachelors of Blair Memorial
In Graywolf's Hands IM #1155
M.D. Most Wanted IM #1167
Mac's Bedside Manner SE #1492
Undercover M.D. IM #1191

Two Halves of a Whole
The Baby Came C.O.D. SR #1264
Desperately Seeking Twin Yours Truly

Those Sinclairs
Holding Out for a Hero IM #496
Heroes Great and Small IM #501
Christmas Every Day IM #538
Caitlin's Guardian Angel IM #661

The Cutlers of the Shady Lady Ranch
(Yours Truly titles)
Fiona and the Sexy Stranger
Cowboys Are for Loving
Will and the Headstrong Female
The Law and Ginny Marlow
A Match for Morgan
A Triple Threat to Bachelorhood SR #1564

*The Reeds
Callaghan's Way IM #601
Serena McKee's Back in Town IM #808

*McClellans & Marinos
Man Trouble SR #815
The Taming of the Teen SR #839
Babies on His Mind SR #920
The Baby beneath the Mistletoe SR #1408

*The Alaskans
Wife in the Mail SE #1217
Stand-In Mom SE #1294
Found: His Perfect Wife SE #1310
The M.D. Meets His Match SE #1401
Lily and the Lawman SE #1467

*The Pendletons
Baby in the Middle SE #892
Husband: Some Assembly Required SE #931

The Mom Squad
A Billionaire and a Baby SE #1528
A Bachelor and a Baby SD #1503
The Baby Mission IM #1220

*Unflashed series

MARIE FERRARELLA

earned a master's degree in Shakespearean comedy, and, perhaps as a result, her writing is distinguished by humor and natural dialogue. This RITA® Award-winning author's goal is to entertain and to make people laugh and feel good. She has written over one hundred books for Silhouette, some under the name Marie Nicole. Her romances are beloved by fans worldwide and have been translated into Spanish, Italian, German, Russian, Polish, Japanese and Korean.

To
Patience Smith
and our bonding process

Prologue

She was back. He'd seen her. Seen Claire.

Held her.

Her eyes were closed now, but she knew it was him. He knew she knew. Because Claire was his.

Now and forever.

He'd been away for three long, aching years and when he'd finally been allowed to return, he was afraid that he'd never see her again. That she would be gone.

But he had found her, found Claire. No one else would ever have her again. Would ever touch her again.

There were no words to do justice to the emotions that were skittering through him. Elation, joy, empowerment, those were all good words, but not really good enough. Not nearly good enough to begin to describe what it was he was experiencing right at this moment, just looking at her lying here on the grass.

He sifted a strand of her hair through his fingers. Bending down, he closed his eyes for a moment and inhaled deeply.

Her hair smelled of something herbal. Something nice.

Silky blond hair.

Hair that would continue to grow even though she no longer would. She wouldn't have the promise of another sunrise, another star-filled night.

He sat back on his heels and looked at her.

She looked so beautiful.

In his other hand, he held a rose. A single, perfect red rose. A rose as perfect as the young woman who lay here before him.

There were bruises on her throat, which marred that perfection. But he had hidden them. Nobody would ever see.

Carefully he placed the single red rose in her hand, then arranged the fingers of her other hand around the stem. He sat back and studied his handiwork.

She looked as if she was sleeping.

Perfect.

The pressure in his chest was gone. It felt good to be back.

To have Claire again.

Because he loved her.

Chapter 1

"Guess who's back?"

Special Agent Chris Jones, C.J. to her friends, looked up from her desk, the same desk that had kept her a virtual prisoner in the Southern California office for the past two months. She struggled against a very strong inclination to frown.

By the tone of her partner's voice, her completely free-to-work-in-the-field-while-she-withered-on-the-vine-in-the-office partner, Special Agent Byron Warrick was either going to give her more paperwork to cope with, or worse, he had something going on in the field that she was barred from. The powers that be didn't think a pregnant woman belonged out there.

Bracing herself, she tossed her long, straight, blond hair over her shoulder and asked, "Who?"

Warrick perched on the edge of C.J.'s desk and looked down at her. All of her. He hadn't seen her in nearly a week, and every time he was away from her, he had to admit it was a shock when he first saw her again.

He wasn't accustomed to seeing her this way. When they had first been teamed up, she'd weighed scarcely more than his equipment bag for the pee-wee softball team he used to coach. The last couple of months had certainly taken their toll on his partner.

He shook his head. She dressed well, and there was a certain amount of camouflage involved, but there was no way she could hide what was going on.

Warrick stole a peppermint from her desk and began to remove the cellophane. ''You know, C.J., I can't remember what you looked like when you weren't pregnant.''

Why was it that men felt compelled to bury affection in a sea of banter, barbs and teasing? There were times when Warrick acted just like one of her brothers.

''Very funny.'' C.J. sighed, then admitted, ''Neither can I.'' She pushed the keyboard back on her desk. Something was clearly up. ''Okay, what has you so all-fired chipper this morning?''

''Not chipper, C.J.'' Under the circumstances, that was rather a disrespectful word to apply to the situation, but then, she didn't know yet. ''Just energized.''

He played out the moment, reeling C.J. in. He felt

bad for her, knowing how she felt about being stuck behind a desk. But he also felt relieved. Her reflexes had to have slowed down in this condition, and he didn't want to have to be worried about something happening to her if she tried to go about business as usual. Business was definitely *not* as usual.

"Remember our old friend, the Sleeping Beauty Killer?"

Recall was instant. C.J. stiffened. The Sleeping Beauty Killer was the name she had dubbed the serial killer who had killed twelve women over the space of two years. All his victims were blue-eyed blondes, all between the ages of twenty and thirty. The name had been given him not for any missives the killer had left in his wake, but for the way he had arranged all the bodies postmortem. He strangled his victims, put a costume jewelry choker on them to hide the marks on their necks and then lyrically placed them on the ground with their hands folded around a single long-stemmed, perfect red rose. The women all appeared as if they were just sleeping, waiting for their prince to come and wake them up with a kiss.

Except that no kiss could undo what he had done to them.

Ordinarily, since all the murders had taken place in the vicinity of Orange County, the FBI wouldn't have gotten involved unless requested to do so by the local authorities. But victim number two had been found in the parking lot of the federal court building. That made it a federal case and gave the

Bureau primary jurisdiction. She'd been the first to come aboard.

Capturing the Sleeping Beauty Killer had been C.J.'s own personal crusade, one that had gone unfulfilled. The killings had abruptly stopped three years ago and the trail had gone completely dry.

The drudgery of the morning with its data inputting was forgotten. C.J.'s eyes brightened as she looked up at Warrick.

"Are you sure?" She made no attempt to hide the eagerness in her voice. If the serial killer was back, that instantly increased their chances of finally getting him for all the murders. "As far as anyone knows, he's been out of commission for three years."

The unofficial theory was that someone had turned the tables on the Sleeping Beauty Killer and killed him. Serial killers rarely lost the blood lust, so the abrupt termination hadn't been voluntary. C.J. had spent countless hours scouring the crime databases herself, looking for any murders that had been committed using a similar MO. But none had come to light. Eventually C.J. decided, with no small relief, that although she wasn't the one to bring him to justice, chances were that the Sleeping Beauty Killer was answering to a higher power for his crimes.

Obviously, relief had been premature, she thought.

"Take a look at what just came in." Separating the photograph from the rest of the folder he was carrying, Warrick tossed it on her desk.

C.J.'s stomach tightened. She found herself looking down at an angelic face that was all but devoid of makeup. The Sleeping Beauty Killer liked them fresh, untouched by anything but death.

The girl in the photograph couldn't have been more than twenty. Her whole life ahead of her, and now it was gone. With effort C.J. pushed down the anger that rose up within her.

She took the photograph in her hands, studying it. The girl was holding a single red rose in her hands. It was too eerily similar. But there were the three years to consider.

C.J. raised her eyes to Warrick's face. "Copycat?" Not that that was a cause for celebration. Copycat or original, the girl was still dead.

"Maybe." But somehow Warrick doubted it. He tapped the folder. "But he got it right, down to the last detail. Including the polished pink nails."

It was the one detail they'd withheld from the public when the story had broken. The Sleeping Beauty Killer liked to give the women he strangled a manicure, also postmortem. He used the same shade of nail polish every time, a shade too common to be useful in their search.

C.J. shivered. "Sick bastard," she muttered under her breath. In an unguarded moment, her hand slipped down over her belly in the eternal protective movement of expectant mothers everywhere, as if trying to shield her baby from this kind of horror. *It's not the best place I'm bringing you into, baby.* She let the photograph drop back on her desk. "I

guess he isn't rotting in hell the way he was supposed to be.''

Warrick tucked the photograph back into the
folder. "Guess not.''

C.J.'s eyes were drawn back to the photograph.
They had to catch this killer before he struck again.
She tried not to think about how many other times
she'd thought the same thing. "Okay, what have we
got on this?''

There was that word again, Warrick thought. *We.*
They weren't a ''we'' at the moment. And they
wouldn't be until after her baby was born. She made
things hard on both of them by not remembering
that fact.

"Information's just coming in, C.J.'' Looking at
her, he could read her mind the way only some
members of her family could. They'd been partners
for six years now, covered each other's backs on the
job and offered silent support outside the job's pe-
rimeters when the situation called for it. "Hey, this
isn't a signal to leap out from behind your desk.''
His green eyes swept over her considerable bulk as
a hint of a smile played on his lips. "Not that leaping appears to be in your repertoire at the moment.''

"Thanks a bunch.'' C.J. shifted in her seat, wishing she could get comfortable, knowing it was a futile effort. These days *comfortable* was only a word
in the dictionary. "I wasn't about to leap, just walk
out with as much dignity as a pregnant elephant can
muster.''

He'd crossed the line and hurt her feelings, Warrick realized. So he backtracked a little. "I wouldn't say elephant."

"Not verbally," C.J. countered, knowing she had him and skewering him just a little. Because he owed it to her. "But I can see what you're thinking in your eyes. I always could, you know."

He liked being able to read her, but he didn't like being transparent himself. "What I'm thinking is that any normal woman would have already gone on maternity leave by now."

She'd been over this subject ad nauseum, with both Warrick and her family. Four brothers, two parents and a partner, all of whom thought they knew better than she did what was best for her.

"We both know I don't fall into that category," C.J. reminded him. "And we superwomen have an image to maintain."

He grinned. It was the kind of grin that raised women's blood pressures and lowered their resistance. At times, C.J. mused, it was hard to remember that she thought of him as another brother and was thus immune to him. He did have one hell of a smile. Lately she kept finding herself attracted to her partner at very odd moments. For some reason, Warrick had been looking sexier and sexier to her. Had to be the hormones, she decided. They were completely out of kilter. She was usually better at keeping a tight rein on her thoughts.

"Superwoman, huh?" Warrick nodded at her stomach. "I don't exactly picture you flying around right about now."

She eyed the folder in his hands. It was like waving a piece of ham in front of a starving dog. "Did you just come in here with this to torture me?"

Following her eyes, he tucked the folder under his arm. "No, but it was our case. I thought you'd want to be in the loop."

Impatient, she shifted in her chair again. It creaked its protest over the change of position. C.J. frowned. "These days I feel like the whole damn loop."

One more month, she thought, squelching a note of desperation. One more month like this and then it'd be over. One more month and she'd have this baby so she could try to get her life back on track again. It was going to be a lot better when she could finally hold her baby in her arms instead of carrying it around like a leaden weight.

She tried not to let her mind drift. There was time enough for maternal feelings *after* the baby arrived, healthy and strong. Until then, she was determined to keep her emotions under tight wrap.

That wasn't going very well right now.

C.J. noted where her partner's eyes were resting. On her abdomen. Annoyance rose up three flights.

"Don't look at me like that. I've got my whole family watching my stomach as if it's a pot about to boil, and I don't need my partner doing the same thing."

Warrick straightened. "The person you should have watching your stomach is—"

She shut her eyes, searching for a vein of strength. They'd been down this road before, too. Too often.

"Don't start, War. I know what you're going to say and I don't want to hear it."

"Don't want to hear what?" He meant to make his question sound innocent. It sounded heated instead. But he wasn't exactly impartial when it came to the FBI special agent who, until seven months ago, had a prominent place in his partner's life—a partner he was extremely fond of. If he felt anything else toward her, well, that was something that wasn't going to be explored in the light of day. It couldn't be. Never mind that, pregnant or not, C.J. was the hottest-looking woman he'd ever come across. "That your insignificant other should at least be around to lend you some emotional support?"

They'd already been through this, she and Warrick. Why couldn't he get this through his thick black Irish head? "He's not my 'other' anything, War."

The hell the man wasn't. He had no idea what the attraction had been, but it was obviously hot enough to get her in this condition. Hot enough for her to want to keep the baby instead of going another route.

Restless, Warrick got up. "I just think that after he got you pregnant—"

C.J. took instant offense. From the moment she'd first opened her eyes on the world, despite the fact that she had a warm, loving family, she'd been her own person. She resented the implication, even for a moment, that she wasn't.

"Nobody *got* me anything. We took precautions, they didn't work. The pregnancy was an accident."

Again her hand went over her belly, as if to block out any hurtful words the baby might hear. "It happens, okay? Now if you don't mind, Special Agent Warrick, let's drop the subject."

She watched the deep frown take root on his face and tried to tell herself she appreciated where he was coming from. He just cared about her, the way she did about him. Cared the way she had when his wife of two years had left him three years ago because she couldn't stand the instability of the life he led.

"Don't talk to me like that, C.J., as if we're two characters out of the *X-Files,* calling to each other by our titles. It's not natural. And neither," he added vehemently, "is walking away from a woman you're supposed to be in love with."

He'd never liked Tom Thorndyke, hadn't liked him from the first moment the man had stared unabashedly at C.J. But he'd made concessions because C.J. obviously cared about the jerk. He hated to see her hurt and abandoned. For two cents proper, he'd make the man eat his perfect teeth. If he could get to him. The man had taken an assignment out of the state right after he'd told C.J. that they were better off going their separate ways.

Which was right after she'd told him she was pregnant.

"Forget about Tom Thorndyke and tell me who's been assigned to the case." C.J. shrugged. She'd made up her mind to only look ahead and not back. Looking back never got you anywhere, anyway.

Because he knew they weren't going to get anywhere waltzing over old ground, Warrick backed off and told her what she wanted to know. "Rodriguez, Culpepper…"

The two other special agents who had been on the original task force. A flutter of unfounded hope passed through her. "And?"

"Me."

C.J. knew what he was telling her. Disappointment jabbed her with a sharp, extra-long knitting needle. "But not me."

He'd gone to bat to get her on the team over the assistant director's reservations. On the team safely. "Unofficially." Warrick pointed to the computer. "You can cross-check information for us, go through the files, things like that."

It wasn't what she wanted to hear. "I've got too much seniority to be a grunt, Warrick, and I'm not old enough to be stuck behind a computer."

He looked at her for a long moment. She should never have gotten involved with that character. For once it seemed as if her keen instincts had completely failed her. "Should have thought of that before you tripped the light fantastic with old shoot-and-scoot."

She'd never been long on patience. Pregnancy had cut her lag time in half. She struggled to hold on to her temper. "Don't you think it's about time you stopped with the cute references?"

"I'll stop when he materializes out of the Bermuda Triangle to live up to his end of it." He looked at her long and hard. "And there's nothing 'cute' about a man who ducks out on his responsibilities."

She'd given the matter a great deal of thought

even before she'd told Thorndyke about the baby she was carrying. She'd found herself drawing up a list of the man's pros and cons. Disgusted, she'd crumpled them up. Love and marriage was not decided by a safe, sane list of pros and cons, but on a gut feeling, a lack of breath and an X-factor that defied description. None of the latter applied to Tom Thorndyke. The relationship, short as it was, had been a mistake. A misjudgment on her part because she'd been lonely, and she took full responsibility for it.

She just wished Warrick would let it drop. "The worst thing in the world would have been for Thorndyke and me to get married."

Part of him felt that way, too. But he wasn't about to tell her that. "If you felt that way, why did you sleep with him?"

Very simply because she hadn't thought about any consequences arising from the liaison. For once in her life, impulse had guided her. But once she'd discovered she was pregnant, changes in her outlook followed. She saw Tom's true colors. And maternal instincts came out of nowhere. She never once doubted that she wanted this baby. But even so, she refused to allow herself the luxury of making plans. Plans had a way of falling through, dragging disappointment in their wake.

She looked at Warrick. "Since when do I owe you any explanations?"

Holding the folder in one hand, he opened his arms wide and shrugged. "You don't." With that, he turned away.

Annoyed at him and herself, C.J. called after him. "You can have a serving of ice cream without wanting to marry the ice cream vat." Warrick stopped and looked at her over his shoulder. She shrugged. "Besides, it was just one of those things that happened. It would be a mistake to have three people pay for one night of passion." And a birth control method that had failed, she added silently.

He crossed back to her slowly. "I guess that makes sense."

She'd known all along that Warrick hadn't liked Tom. Maybe, in some perverse way, that might have even spurred her on, although she couldn't have actually explained why. In any event, as far as she was concerned that was all behind her.

"Okay, enough atonement, Father Warrick." She put her hand out for the folder. "Give me the information. Do we know who the victim is?"

He nodded. There'd been no mystery here. "Same as always." Warrick handed her the folder. "There was a wallet. He doesn't get his jollies challenging us."

As far as serial killers went, the Sleeping Beauty Killer wasn't unduly cruel. He'd always made a point of making sure that the victim could be readily identified, that her next of kin, if there were any, could easily be contacted and informed of the person's death. The only secrecy was his identity. And why he killed in the first place.

C.J. glanced at the information. She felt heartsick for the family. No one should have to put up with this kind of thing happening.

"A serial killer with heart. How lovely. Damn it, Warrick." She slapped the folder down on her desk. "I want this guy in the worst way." Emotions weren't going to catch the killer. Only cold, hard, deliberate investigation would do it. And a great deal of luck. "What do you think made him stop for so long?"

He perched on her desk again. She was wearing a different perfume, he noted. It was sexier. He couldn't help wondering if she was trying to compensate for her present state. At a different time...

He caught his thoughts before they could slip off to somewhere they shouldn't.

"Maybe he didn't. Maybe he just shifted his base of operations," he theorized. "Maybe our guy discovered that the world is a hell of a lot larger than just Orange County in California."

It was a theory, but not one she subscribed to. Not after all the hours she'd logged in, looking for the Sleeping Beauty Killer's pattern and coming up empty. "I don't think so. No other murders matched this particular, meticulous MO. No, something made him stop. How do you crawl into the head of someone like this?" she wondered out loud.

He looked at her. There was a danger in that. "Careful that once you crawl in, you don't forget how to crawl out again."

She laughed, knowing exactly what he was referring to. "Been watching Al Pacino in *Cruising* again?" Though he denied it, the award-winning actor was clearly one of Warrick's favorites.

"Hey, things like that happen," he protested.

"You become one with the criminal and forget where you end off and he starts."

She shivered. "Never happen. There's no way I would ever mentally bond with this character. He gives me the creeps." Just touching the folder made her skin crawl. He had to get these women to trust him, played on their vulnerability and then struck. He was a loathsome creature of the lowest order.

Warrick was more concerned about her right now than the Sleeping Beauty Killer. "Why don't you knock it off for a while?" He glanced at his watch. It was close to two. If he didn't miss his guess, she hadn't left her desk, except for bathroom runs, since she'd come in this morning. "Want to pick up some late lunch?"

She tilted her head, studying his face, suppressing a grin. "You buying?"

"No way." Warrick laughed shortly. "I've seen the way you eat lately. We'll go Dutch." He moved behind her. "I will, however, help you out of your chair."

Another crack, however veiled, about her weight. She could do without that, even though she'd gained a good twenty-eight pounds in the past two months. Before then, she'd stayed rail thin, actually losing weight because of an extra-long bout of morning sickness.

"Forever the gentleman. Thanks," she waved him away, "but I'll pass." She opened the folder and spread it out on her desk. "I want to go through this file."

Serial killers were not something a woman about

to give birth should be concentrating on. Maybe that made him old-fashioned, he mused.

"You know, you could start thinking about decorating that spare bedroom of yours." He knew from her brothers that she still hadn't bought a single thing to reflect her pending motherhood.

C.J. looked at him sharply. Not him, too. He was the last one she would have thought would bother her about this. "Bad luck."

He shook his head. "I never took you to be the superstitious type."

Her shoulders rose and fell in a vague gesture. "We're all superstitious in our own way." It had taken her time to come to terms with this phase of her life, but now she wanted this baby, wanted it badly. And was afraid of wanting it. "I don't like counting on anything unless it's right there in front of me."

Her comment surprised him. It wasn't like her. "I thought I was supposed to be the cynical one."

Her smile went straight to his inner core. It never failed to amaze him how connected he and this woman were. Even more so than he and his wife had been. As a rule he wasn't given to close relationships, always keeping a part of himself in reserve. But there was something about C.J. that transcended that rule.

"Spend six years with someone," she told him, "some bad habits are bound to rub off. But if you must know, you didn't have anything to do with this one. My mother's four aunts did a number on me once the cat was out of the bag." Aided and abetted by her enduring trim figure, it had taken her five months to tell her family about her condition. They'd been wonderfully supportive, and ever so slightly annoyingly intrusive. "They had a dozen stories about miscarriages to tell me. Each."

He leaned over the desk. A strand of her hair hung in her face, and he tucked it behind her ear. In typical obstinate behavior, she shook her head, causing it to come loose again. He wondered why he found that so damn attractive. He shouldn't.

"You're eight months along and the doctor gave you a clean bill of health. I don't think you have to worry about miscarrying. Just about how to make the spineless wonder pay his fair share."

Warrick was definitely too close—and making odd things happen inside her. C.J. pushed herself away from the desk—and her partner. "Warrick, I know that in your own twisted little way, you care about me. But get this through that thick head of yours. I don't want anything from Tom Thorndyke. As far as I am concerned, this is my baby and only *my* baby."

He crossed his arms before his chest. "Another case of the immaculate conception?"

Her temper was dangerously close to going over to the dark side. "Byron—"

He winced at the sound of his first name. One of these days, when he got a chance to get around to it, he was going to have it legally changed. Lord Byron had been his mother's favorite poet while she was carrying him, but there was no reason that he had to suffer because of that.

"Okay, I'll back off."

"Thank you."

He started to head for the door. "Want me to bring you back anything?"

She glanced at the folder on her desk. "Just the Sleeping Beauty Killer's head on a platter."

He laughed, shaking his head. "Afraid that's not the special of the day." Warrick paused for a moment longer, looking at her. There was affection in his eyes, as well as concern. "Take some personal time."

She just waved him off, then watched appreciatively as he walked away. The man had one hell of a tight butt.

"Damn hormones," she muttered to herself as she began to pore over the folder he had given her.

Her hands braced on the arms of her office chair, C.J. pushed herself up to her feet. It was late, but she wasn't finished yet. Time for her hourly sojourn to the bathroom.

She hated this lumbering girth that had become hers. In top condition since the age of ten when she'd picked up her first free weight to brain her older brother, Brian—an occurrence her father had prevented at the last moment—C.J. hated physical restrictions of any kind. The last two months of her pregnancy had forced her to assume a lifestyle she disliked intensely.

The only thing that made it bearable was knowing that she was doing it for her baby's good. But it was rough being noble, especially as she watched Warrick team up with other people, handling cases she wanted to be handling. She'd never been one to sit on the sidelines and it was killing her.

"Ah, I see you're ready to go."

Turning around, C.J. saw Diane Jones coming toward her. She didn't remember making any arrangements to meet her mother at the office. "What are you doing here?"

"Is that any way to greet your mother?" Diane pressed a quick kiss to her daughter's temple. "Ethan had a deposition to take not far from here. He dropped me off." She tapped her wristwatch. "Chris, your Lamaze class starts in half an hour. At this time of day, it might take us that long to get there. Let's go."

She'd only gotten halfway through the details in the reports. Besides, she wasn't in the mood to stretch and lie on the floor. Class wasn't as much fun now that Sherry and Joanna were gone, each having given birth.

"I was thinking of not going," she told her mother.

Protests had never gotten in Diane's way. She hooked her arm through her daughter's, tugging her in the direction of the door.

"Fine. And you can continue thinking about it on the way there." She used her "mom" voice, the one that had allowed her to govern four energetic boys and a daughter whose energy level went off the charts. "Let's go, Chris. Don't make me get Warrick in here to convince you."

Funny how much a part of her family her partner had become. "He's out in the field."

Diane picked up on her daughter's tone. "You'll be out there, giving me heart failure, soon enough." She gave C.J.'s arm another tug. "Now let's go."

Resigned, C.J., sighed and got her purse from the bottom desk drawer. "Yes, Mother."

Diane nodded, pleased at the capitulation. "Well, it could be a little more cheerful, but I'll take what I can get."

So saying, she gently pushed her daughter out the door.

"We have to stop at the bathroom," C.J. told her.

Diane's smile didn't fade. "I never doubted it for a minute."

Chapter 2

"I've got a surprise for you," Lamaze instructor Lori O'Neill whispered to C.J. as the class began breaking up.

Handing her pillow to her mother, C.J. looked at the perky, rather pregnant blond instructor. The session had run a little long tonight. All C.J. wanted to do was drop her mother off at her house and go home herself.

She'd been preoccupied throughout the entire session, her mind constantly reverting to some stray piece of information about one or another of the Sleeping Beauty Killer's victims. Twice her mother'd had to tap her on her shoulder to get her to pay attention to what was going on in class.

This was a far cry from the way the classes normally used to go, Lori thought. It wasn't all that long

ago that she, Lori, Sherry Campbell and Joanna
Prescott would go out together after class to a local,
old-fashioned ice cream parlor where they would in-
dulge their insatiable craving for sweets. But Sherry
and Joanna were no longer part of the class, or the
inner clique Lori had pulled together and whimsi-
cally dubbed the Mom Squad. Sherry and Joanna
had each given birth and with new men in their lives
as well, were on their way to no longer being single
mothers.

C.J. shook her head. "I don't think—"

On a mission of mercy, Lori was not about to take
no for an answer. "You've been looking a little
down these last two sessions, so I called up Sherry
and Joanna and invited them out for the evening.
They're waiting for us at the ice cream parlor."

She really didn't need the extra calories. Even so,
C.J. could feel her taste buds getting into gear. Still,
she felt she needed to review the personal notes
she'd kept at home dealing with the serial killer's
various victims. There just had to be *something* she
was missing.

C.J. grasped at a plausible excuse. "But I've got
to drop off my mother—"

The excuse died quickly. "Not another word
about it," Diane protested. She was already digging
her cell phone out of her purse. "I'll just call your
father and he can come to pick me up." Her blue
eyes sparkled lustily as she grinned at her only
daughter. "Did I ever tell you about the first time
he picked me up?" She sighed dramatically. "Your
father was the handsomest thing on two legs, and I

would have followed him to the ends of the earth.'' She winked at Lori. ''Luckily, I didn't have to. His apartment was right around the corner.''

C.J. had grown up hearing the story in its various forms, originally amended because of her age, then updated on every occasion. In its time, it had made a wonderful bedtime story, but not tonight. She cut her mother off before she could get rolling. ''You don't mind calling him?''

Diane pressed a single number on the cell's keypad. ''Not in the slightest.'' Her eyes took on a glow as a male voice echoed in her ear. ''James? Chris can't drop me off, would you mind coming to get me?'' Catching her daughter's eye, she shook her head tolerantly. ''No, she's not going out in the field.'' Diane covered the cell phone with a well-manicured hand. ''He worries about his little girl,'' she confided to Lori.

C.J. rolled her eyes. ''I'm probably the only FBI agent who has to look over her shoulder to make sure her father isn't trailing after her.'' Her father would have been a great deal happier with her if she'd put her law degree to use and followed him into the firm, as her three older brothers had. Even Jamie, the youngest, was studying law. She was the only maverick in the family—and she liked it that way.

Lori laughed, slipping an arm around C.J.'s shoulders. ''Hey, it's nice having a family care about you. I'd give anything to have my dad trailing after me.'' Both of her parents were gone now. The only family Lori had left was her late husband's older brother.

Diane flipped her phone shut. "There, all settled." She tucked the cell phone into her purse.
"Your father'll be here in fifteen minutes." She
shooed the women off. "Go, have an ice cream for
me." She looked down at a figure that was still trim
by anyone's standards except her own and sighed.
"Anything I eat goes right to my hips. No passing
go, no collecting two hundred dollars, just directly
to my hips."

Lori gave C.J. a quizzical look. C.J. was quick to
provide an explanation. "Mom's a Monopoly en-
thusiast."

Diane leaned in and confided to Lori. "She'd say
'freak' if I wasn't here." The look she gave her
daughter spoke volumes. "We all have our little ob-
sessions."

Her mind on other things, C.J. couldn't help
thinking about the Sleeping Beauty Killer and the
women he had singled out to eliminate. "Yes," she
agreed quietly, "we do."

The ice cream parlor, with its quaint booths and
small tables, looked as if it belonged to another era,
nestled in another century. C.J. felt completely at
ease here. There was something soothing about the
decor. It spoke of innocence and simplicity, something she found herself longing for.

By the time she and Lori arrived, Sherry and
Joanna, both now enviably slim, were already seated
at a booth. Sherry waved to them the moment they
walked in.

There was no need to place an order. The instant

the waitress saw the four of them, she began making notations on her pad. The women's choice almost never varied.

"I'm really glad you called," Sherry told Lori as she settled back with her hot-fudge sundae. "I've been meaning to get in touch." Her eyes swept over the faces of the other two women. "With all of you." Leaving her spoon buried deep within the mountain of French vanilla ice cream, she dug into her purse and pulled out three official-looking ivory envelopes. She handed one to each of them. "I'm not economizing on stamps," she explained. "I just thought the personal touch was nicer."

Taking a generous spoonful of ice cream, Sherry savored the taste as she watched her three friends open up the lacy envelopes.

The tearing of paper was followed by squeals of enthusiasm and mutual joy.

C.J. was the first to collect herself and say something closer to a level pitch. "You're getting married."

Sherry grinned. If anyone had told her three months ago that she would be marrying one of the richest men in the country, not to mention one of the best looking, she would have told them they were crazy. But here she was, wildly in love and engaged. Life had a funny way of working things out with excellent results. "Yeah, I know."

Joanna tucked the invitation away into her purse and began sipping her strawberry ice cream soda in earnest. "Talk about the lengths that a journalist is willing to go to in order to get an exclusive interview…"

A reporter for the *Bedford World News,* Sherry's assignment had begun as a challenge. To get a background story on an elusive, successful corporate raider dubbed Darth Vader. Things had gotten tangled up when she'd suddenly gone into labor at his mountain hideaway. St. John Adair had wound up delivering her baby. From there, everything had just escalated.

Sherry looked at her friends. They all knew her story. She'd become as close to them as she was to her own family.

"*Exclusive* is definitely the key word here." Sherry sighed, temporarily forgetting about the sinful dessert. "I've never felt this way about anyone before." Her grin widened. "Part of me feels that it's got to be illegal to feel this happy."

Reaching over the table, C.J. squeezed her hand. "Enjoy it while you can. As far as I know, they haven't passed a law against that yet."

Since her sundae was beginning to drip a little around the edges, Sherry's attention reverted back to her dessert. "I tried to time the ceremony so that it didn't interfere with either of your due dates." She looked at the two pregnant women. "You will come, won't you?"

She could use a little happy diversion in her life, C.J. thought. "Try and stop me."

Lori patted her stomach affectionately. "Count me in. This little darling'll be out and smiling in time for you to exchange your vows."

"Babies don't smile until they're at least six months old," C.J. contradicted. She saw Lori begin to protest. "Those funny little expressions you see on their faces is just gas."

"Don't you believe it," Joanna interjected with all the confidence of a new first-time mother delving through the mysteries of babies. "My baby smiles at me all the time. And at Rick."

"That's not surprising," Sherry commented. "A stone would smile at Rick." Her eyes shifted toward C.J. The FBI special agent was the next one due and had plied both her and Joanna with questions about what giving birth actually felt like. "So, are you getting excited?"

C.J. had gone from excited to nervous to feeling twinges of encroaching panic. With the big event less than a month away, she was now banking down any and all thoughts regarding the pending experience. It was easier getting through the day that way.

"I'm trying not to think about it." She took a long sip of her mint chocolate-chip shake and let the coolness slide down her throat before continuing. "I'm not much on anticipating pain."

Or dealing with the fear that had descended over her, she added silently. For probably the first time in her life, she found herself afraid of the unknown. Afraid of what she *did* know about the unknown. Afraid of what came after, as well. Because, despite the support of her family and friends, she was afraid of screwing up.

Joanna waved away the comment. "That's just a

small part of it," she assured C.J. "It's true what they say, you know. You do forget."

C.J. curled her lip cynically. "Probably because it hurts so much, you black out."

Lori looked at her in surprise. "I've never heard you sound so negative before." She studied her for a second. "Anything wrong?"

C.J. sighed, pushing her straw into a glob of ice cream. "Just feeling sorry for myself, I guess." She saw the others were waiting for a more detailed explanation. "My partner's out in the field, tracking down a serial killer."

Sherry was the first to break the silence. "Serial-killer envy." Exchanging looks with the others, she laughed incredulously. "Boy, that's definitely not my thing." And then she became serious. "You're a mom-to-be, C.J. You're supposed to be agonizing over what shade of blue or pink to paint the nursery, not about wanting to go chasing after the bad guys with a gun strapped to the inside of your maternity bra."

They didn't understand, C.J. thought. Though she gave the appearance of being flamboyant and quick to act, deep down, she felt a strong commitment to her work. She defined herself by it. There was this overwhelming need within her to put "the bad guys," as Sherry called them, away.

"Speaking of nursery," Joanna, ever the peace-maker, interjected, "*have* you decided to finally let us give you baby presents?"

It was a sore point with everyone, C.J. sensed. Even her brothers were commenting on it. Warrick's crack this afternoon had made it unanimous. She shook her head, a curiously shy smile creeping along her lips. "There's no need to give me presents."

"Yes, there is," Sherry insisted. She waved her hand around the table, taking them all in. "It's part of the bonding process."

Sherry thought back to when they had all initially gotten together. She knew as far as she went, talking with the women had gone a long way toward helping her remain calm about the challenges that were ahead of her. She had her parents, whom she loved dearly, but there was something infinitely comforting about being able to turn to women who were in the exact same rocky boat as she was and be able to talk out the fears that plagued her.

"We're all in this together, so to speak," Sherry pointed out. "C'mon, C.J., why won't you let us give you anything?"

"After," C.J. told them. "Once he or she is here."

This time it was Joanna's turn to shake her head. "I can't believe that you're the only one of the four of us who had an amniocentesis done and you didn't ask the doctor to tell you what you were having."

She had her reasons. "I always liked opening up my gifts at the end of the day, not the beginning."

C.J. didn't add that she was afraid if she knew the sex of the baby, she'd start thinking of it as a real person. This way, if something unforeseeable did happened and she lost the baby, she could still mentally divorce herself from it somehow.

Just the way she had from Tom.

All her protests to Warrick and her family notwithstanding, when Tom told her that he thought it was best if they just stopped seeing each other, she'd felt cruelly disappointed. She'd honestly thought that for once, she'd found someone she could count on. Someone who felt as strongly about her as she did about him.

That was what happened when you expected too much, she told herself. You wound up with too little. Or, in this case, with almost nothing at all.

But she was determined that no one would suspect how she really felt. It didn't go with the image of herself she wanted to project.

Wanting to change the direction of the conversation, she looked at Joanna. "So, your turn. How are things going with you?"

Joanna's eyes glowed. She pushed aside her almost depleted dish of dessert, wiping off the area in front of her. "I thought you'd never ask."

Digging deeply into her purse, she pulled out a small white album that was almost bursting at the seams. It was crammed full of brand-new photographs of her brand-new baby.

Sherry laughed as she dug into her own purse. "I'll meet your stack—" she plunked down her own album "—and raise you five pictures."

"You're on," Joanna declared.

Lori exchanged looks with C.J. "I think we're about to get babied to death."

"Bring them on," C.J. encouraged. "I can't think of a sweeter way to go."

* * *

Last night had been nice break, but it felt good to get back to work, C.J. thought as she sat, reading over the folder that Warrick had left with her yesterday. She was reviewing it for the umpteenth time.

The office was empty, except for her. There were times she welcomed the quiet.

She enjoyed getting together with the other women. That in itself was a constant source of surprise to her. Apart from her mother, she'd been raised in a world of men. With three older brothers and one younger one, C.J. found that she had a difficult time relating to other women.

But Lori, Sherry and Joanna were different. Maybe because, for different reasons, they had all found themselves approaching motherhood while in a single status. Facing the biggest event in their lives without a life partner beside them had given them all something in common.

Something in common.

What did these thirteen women have in common? she wondered, staring down at the photographs spread out on her desk. Beyond the obvious, of course. If you looked quickly, and myopically, they almost looked like photographs of the same person.

Of her, she thought grimly. Because she bore the same eerily similar physical features as the dead women. She was a blue-eyed blonde within the age range that the Sleeping Beauty Killer gravitated toward.

There but for the grace of God…

C.J. shifted uncomfortably in her seat. She didn't

know if it was the thought or the unnerving twinges she kept feeling that was getting to her.

What had made the Sleeping Beauty Killer snuff out these women's lives, executing them politely but firmly? Why them? Why not green-eyed redheads or brown-eyed brunettes?

There had to be a reason. Something.

One by one she held up the photographs of the young women, taken while they were still alive, and examined them closely. Did they represent some kind of fantasy woman to the killer? Someone in his life who had been unattainable to him? Who perhaps had spurned him?

Or was there some kind of other reason behind his choice?

She just didn't know, and not knowing frustrated her to the nth degree. Muttering an oath, she tossed down the last photograph, taken of the last victim. A Bedford University sophomore named Nora Adams.

"Did you know him, Nora? Did you talk to him? Smile at him? Or did you not even see him?"

"Don't you have a home to go to?"

Startled, C.J. almost jumped. It took a moment for her heart to stop slamming against her rib cage. Turning around, she saw that Warrick was standing not five feet away from her. She hadn't even heard him come in.

C.J. took a deep breath and gathered the photographs together again. "Since when did you decide to become my keeper?"

As if that was possible. "It's a dirty job, but someone has to do it."

This pending motherhood with all its emotional baggage was getting her too jumpy, she thought disparagingly. Her nerves felt scattered and dangerously close to the surface. She just wished she didn't ache so. "How's the investigation going?"

He'd been on his way home when he'd decided to take a detour and stop at the field office. He had a hunch C.J. would still be here. There were times, such as these, when he felt that his partner didn't have the common sense of a flea. Not when it came to herself, anyway.

Warrick shoved his hands into his pockets. The case was as frustrating to him as it was to her. There were dead ends as far as the eye could see. Just like the last time.

"No more dead girls, if that's what you're asking. No more clues, either. No fingerprints, no bodily fluids, no sloppy anything left in his wake." He laughed shortly. "It's like the guy's a ghost."

He'd put into words the thought she'd just been entertaining. "Maybe he is."

Warrick looked at her sharply. "What do you mean, like Casper?"

"No." He knew she didn't mean that, C.J. thought in exasperation. "Like someone nobody notices. One of those people who pass through our lives who we never take any note of." Caught up in a fast-paced existence, she was as guilty as everyone else. "The kid bagging your groceries, the toll booth guy making change. The postal worker who weighs your package. People we see every day without really seeing them at all.''

She could be on to something. That could explain why no one ever noticed anyone out of the ordinary hanging around, Warrick reasoned. ''That doesn't mean he won't make a mistake.''

She sighed, flipping the folder closed. She shifted again. Her back was aching in the worst way. She tried to remember if she'd done something to strain it. ''He hasn't until now.''

''And odds are, he won't tonight.''

She looked at Warrick quizzically. What was that supposed to mean? Had he heard something? ''Tonight?''

''Yes.'' Pulling her chair back from her desk, he turned it around to face him and leaned over her. ''Go home, C.J. You look tired.''

Feet planted on the floor, she scooted back. ''Bad lighting.''

There was no such thing as bad lighting as far as C.J. was concerned. She looked good in shadow and in sunlight. Rousing his thoughts, he waved around the office. ''Everyone else is gone.''

She raised her chin defiantly, knowing she was baiting him and enjoying it. ''You're not.''

''That's because I'm checking in on you.'' He stopped, knowing this was going to go nowhere. With C.J. it never did unless she wanted it to. ''God, but you are a stubborn woman.''

She pulled up another program on her computer. Maybe a fresh perspective would help. ''Wouldn't have lasted all this time with you if I wasn't.''

"Hey, the only reason we're together is because I'm the patient one. You're the one who's always running off half-cocked."

The ache began to sear through her body. "No running tonight," she muttered.

He gave it one more try. "C'mon, C.J., let me take you home."

She splayed her hand over her chest. "Why, Warrick, this is so sudden."

Not really. The small voice in his head came out of nowhere, implying things it had no business implying. Damn it, what had gotten into him tonight?

He raised a brow at the wordplay. "Your home, not mine, partner."

It was late and she didn't know how much longer her energy would last. Maybe something she came up with here would ultimately save someone. "Later."

He felt the edge of his temper sharpening. "Now."

C.J. looked away from her screen, fluttering her eyelashes at him. "You're not the boss of me, Warrick."

He gave up. Drop-dead gorgeous or not, she was stubborn as a smelly mule. "Fine, sound like a two-year-old. You'll be good company for that baby of yours."

She knew he meant well, but so did she. There was a man out there killing women because they looked like real-live versions of Barbie, and she had to put a stop to it. "I don't feel like going home, War. There's a stack of dirty dishes in the sink waiting for me, and a pile of laundry held over from the Spanish Civil War. If I'm here, I don't feel guilty about not cleaning.''

She had to be the most contrary woman he'd ever met. Nothing about her went by the book. ''Aren't you supposed to be in the nesting mode by now?''

She hated that term. ''In case you haven't noticed, I'm a woman, not a bird.''

''You're a walking contradiction of terms is what you are.'' Surrendering, Warrick sighed. ''Never could get you to listen to reason.''

She spared him a look and grinned. ''Right, why start now?''

Why indeed. There was a cold beer in his refrigerator with his name on it. It was time to start the reunion. ''Good night, C.J.''

''Uh-huh.'' Her attention was already fastened to the reports she knew almost by heart.

Warrick had crossed the room and was about to pass the threshold when he heard a strange little gasp behind him.

''Warrick?''

There was something in her voice that made the hair on the back of his neck rise up. He swung around to look at her. C.J. was still sitting at her desk, but there was an odd expression on her face.

''What?''

Oh, God. Her words came out measured. ''How close would you say we were?''

That was a hell of an odd question for one partner to ask another. ''Pretty close, I guess.'' He looked at her more intently. ''Why?''

She caught her lower lip between her teeth a second before answering. "I think we're about to get a lot closer."

Like a man feeling his way along a tightrope, Warrick slowly made his way back into the room, staring at C.J. as he came. "What are you talking about?"

Very deliberately C.J. closed the folder on her desk. The pain shot through her again. She fisted her hands against it, but it didn't help. Her knuckles felt as if they were going to break through her skin.

It matched the sensation going on in other parts of her.

She looked up at him, telling herself not to panic. "I'm in labor."

Warrick's eyes widened in disbelief. C.J. was given to practical jokes. This had to be one of them, although it went beyond the pale as far as he was concerned. "The hell you're not."

She caught her breath, trying to keep her voice steady. From everything she'd been able to pull out of Joanna and Sherry, this was definitely the real thing. Her skirt was damp and that could only mean one thing. Her water had broken.

"The hell I am."

Chapter 3

"This isn't funny, Jones," Warrick snapped as a wave of uneasiness all but drowned him. He couldn't remember any incident in his career, recent or otherwise, that had ever had him feeling this unprepared.

The pain found her and began twisting her in two. C.J. tried to fill her lungs with air, but even that hurt. "I don't think any stand-up comic ever gave birth for laughs."

He didn't like the edgy note in her voice. The hope that this was just a bad joke on her part faded. "You're serious."

She pressed her lips together as she looked at him. She felt fear taking a strong toehold. *Don't panic, don't panic.* "Deadly."

"You're really in labor." Somehow, maybe because he didn't want it to, the thought just refused to penetrate his mind.

She nodded her head. Damn, this was *really* beginning to hurt. "Like a prisoner at Devil's Island."

Why was she still just sitting there, gripping both armrests as if she expected the chair to somehow launch her? "Well, damn it, what are you waiting for?" He put his hand on her arm. "Let's go."

She didn't budge. She was afraid to. Afraid to even move. C.J. raised her eyes to his. "That's just the problem, Warrick, all systems *are* go."

Then why wasn't she getting up? This wasn't making any sense. Maybe it *was* a practical joke after all. He'd seen her deadpan her way through more than one joke before. He gave her arm another tug, surprised at how tightly she continued clinging to the armrests.

"Quit fooling around, C.J. The faster we get you to a hospital, the better."

Biting down on her lower lip, C.J. pushed herself upright and immediately sank down in the chair again. Her legs had buckled, giving way beneath her. She couldn't walk, couldn't move.

She looked up at Warrick. "New plan."

Impatience waltzed with nerves. "What?"

She shook her head, shrugging his hand off her arm. "We need a new plan. I can't walk."

This was bad, he thought, becoming really concerned. C.J. just wasn't the frail, damsel-in-distress type. She'd been shot once and had almost snapped off his head when he'd tried to help her up off the ground.

His mind scrambled to make sense of this new input. "Okay, okay, I'll carry you—"

"No!" With a sweeping motion, C.J. batted away his hands and then grabbed onto the arms of the chair again. It was either that or rip his arms out of their sockets. The pain was back and it had brought friends. "You don't understand. It's too late for that."

Did labor enfeeble a woman's brain? She was talking nonsense. "Too late for carrying?"

Breathing and talking at the same time suddenly became a challenge. "Too late...for...anything. I'm having this...bay-BEE."

The sudden crescendo echoed in his head, hurting his ears. "Yes, I know—"

Her efforts to the contrary, panic was definitely taking hold. C.J. looked at him. Did she have to explain everything?

"Now, Warrick...I'm having...it *now*."

He stared at her, numb. "What do you mean 'now'?" She couldn't possibly mean what he thought she was saying. "As in this minute?"

The wave of pain ebbed back a few inches, letting her catch her breath. Perspiration was beginning to drench her. "I knew...if...you...sounded out the... letters, you'd...get...it."

Feeling a little weak himself, Warrick sank down on his knees beside the chair, holding on to one armrest. "C.J., you can't be having this baby now."

"That's...not...what the...baby...thinks. It's breaking...*OUT*." This time, C.J. did grab Warrick's hand. Wrapping her fingers around it tightly, she squeezed and held on for all she was worth. "Oh…God…Warrick, I think…I'm having…an…exorcism."

He felt completely powerless and lost. This was not covered in any FBI handbook he'd ever read. "What do you want me to do?"

C.J.'s answer came without hesitation. "Kill me."

Unequal to what was happening, Warrick dragged his hand through his hair, momentarily at a loss. "Damn it, C.J., this would have never happened if you had better taste in men."

It was lessening, the pain was lessening. C.J. took a breath and hoped her heart wouldn't pop out of her chest. She spared her partner an annoyed look. "What…you saying? A better…class of man…wouldn't…have slept…with me?"

"No." Warrick shot her a look. She knew better than that. She knew he thought she was too good for the likes of Thorndyke, even if he hadn't told her. "I don't know what I'm saying."

He dragged his hand through his hair again, trying to think. Nothing came. He didn't know the first thing to do in this case, other than to keep her from panicking. But it wasn't easy, not when he felt like panicking himself.

"I've got a law degree, C.J., not a degree in babies. I don't know what to do." He took a couple of deep breaths, trying to gather his thoughts together. A small bud of hope began to bloom. "Maybe you're just having false labor."

She felt as if someone had taken a carving knife

to her. "If this is…false…labor, I don't…want…to be around…for the real…thing."

Comfortable, he had to get her comfortable. The thought was almost laughable, seeing the situation. Warrick stripped off his jacket and threw it on the floor. She could lie down on that.

Unbuttoning his sleeves, he pushed them up his forearms. "Okay, let's get you in a better position."

C.J. pressed her lips together, struggling hard not to give in to the waves of panic that were surfing atop waves of pain. "I bet you…say that…to all…the girls."

Determined to muster a small ounce of dignity, she tried to get out of the chair herself. Dignity took a holiday. C.J. all but slid out of the chair in a single fluid motion, landing on his jacket on the floor.

Warrick gave his jacket a couple of tugs, trying to get it flat beneath her and make her more comfortable. It was a futile effort. He knew C.J. wasn't going to be anywhere near comfortable until this baby had made its appearance in the world.

He was in over his head.

Warrick pulled out his cell phone. "I'm calling security—"

Her hand went around his wrist like a steel band. She didn't want some stranger gawking at her while she writhed in pain. She wanted Warrick.

"No…no security." She gave his wrist another tug. "Just…you."

She had entirely too much faith in him, he thought. "C.J., I don't think I can—"

She wouldn't let him finish. Her eyes, filled with

pain, pinned him. "You're…my best friend…Warrick. You've got…to help me…. You can…do this."

Entirely too much faith. Surrendering, Warrick flipped the phone closed. "Yeah, you've got the tough part." He tucked the cell phone back into his pocket and drew closer to her. His voice was calmer when he spoke. If she could have that much faith in him, the least he could do was come through for her. "Okay, C.J., this is all supposed to be natural. What's your body telling you to do?"

She grit her teeth together. "Run…like…hell." And then her eyes opened wide like two huge sunflowers. "I've got…to…push!"

He knew very little about the birth process, but what he did know was that things were happening much too soon. "Are you supposed to do that yet?"

"Dilated," she suddenly remembered. "I'm…supposed to…be…dilated."

Warrick had heard the term in reference to childbirth before, but for the life of him, he wasn't sure what that actually meant. "C.J.?"

The look on his face told her everything. "I'm supposed…to be…fully…opened."

That didn't help very much. Warrick sat back on his heels and looked at her. "I don't know what you look like fully closed, C.J."

Her head ached. It was hard remembering everything that Lori had told them in class. Hard to think at all. Her brain felt as if it was winking in and out. What were the words Lori had used?

"You're...supposed to see...the crown...of...the baby's head." That was it. Crowning. Lori had called it crowning.

A sinking feeling was taking up residence in the pit of his stomach. "Where?"

She stared at Warrick incredulously. When she needed him most, he'd become a complete idiot. "Where...do you...think?"

He knew exactly where he was supposed to look, he'd just been hoping against hope that he was wrong. They'd shared thoughts, feelings, almost everything over the past six years, and he would have been lying if he'd said that the thought of being intimate with her hadn't crossed his mind more than once. But this wasn't the way he wanted to see her nude.

"Oh, God."

The groan escaped before he could prevent it.

The next moment he got a hold of himself. He was all she had right now and he knew it.

In its own way, this was really no different from him having her back when they were out in the field on a dangerous assignment. C.J. was putting her life in his hands and he had to keep her safe—her and this baby of hers who obviously didn't have any respect for due dates.

He offered her what he hoped was an encouraging smile. "You know, when they first put us together, I used to wonder what it would be like if I'd met you on the outside." His smile broadened a little. "This wasn't what I had in mind."

This was no time for them to go to places they couldn't afford to go to. "War—rick."

He took a deep breath, then stated the obvious because he needed to get it out in the open and out of the way. This wasn't going to be easy for either one of them. "It's going to have to get personal."

Damn it, didn't he think she knew that? They weren't waiting for the baby to come COD by parcel post. "Warrick...do what...you...have to do...before... I start ripping off...pieces...of your body...along... with mine."

He grinned this time. "Nice to know you haven't lost your winsome ways. Hang in there, champ."

As delicately as possible, Warrick lifted her skirt and removed her underwear. The moment he did, she raised her hips off the floor, crying out as another contraction, the biggest one so far, seized her in its jaws, tightening around her so hard she thought she was going to snap in two.

She wasn't fooling around, he thought. She was really going to give birth. It was really happening right here on the seventh floor of the federal building.

"I think this is it," he told her, his voice slightly in awe.

"That's...what...I've been...trying...to tell...you!" She twisted and turned, desperately trying to maneuver beyond the pain, and failing. She began to pant hard, not knowing what else to do. The urge to push was overwhelming, and Lori had promised she couldn't pant and push at the same time.

She was panting. What did that mean? Warrick called up every relevant medical program he'd ever watched, trying his best to fathom his next step. The first aid course he'd taken as a teenager had completely faded from his memory banks.

Instincts took over. Needing to reassure her that it was going to be all right, he made his voice become deadly calm. "On the count of three, C.J., I want you to push. One—two—"

She wasn't about to wait on any lousy numbers. She couldn't pant anymore. Sitting bolt upright, she squeezed her eyes shut and bore down.

"Now!" she cried.

Ready or not, she was pushing, he realized. "Damn it, C.J., you never could take instructions." Mentally he counted off the numbers until he reached eight, then looked up at her. Her face beet red, she looked as if she was going to pass out. "Okay, stop, C.J., stop!"

Like a rag doll whose stuffing had been yanked out, C.J. collapsed in a heap on the floor, panting. She felt as if she'd just run one leg of a marathon. Without securing the baton.

Maybe she was wrong. Maybe she'd pushed the baby out and just didn't know it. "Is it—"

"No, not yet."

And then another contraction came, again threatening to tear her in two. She didn't know if she could take much more of this.

She heard the sound of Warrick's voice and strained to make out the words.

"Ready?" he asked. She was breathing hard, as

if she just couldn't pull enough air into her lungs. He glanced up to see if she'd heard him. She was nodding. Just barely. "From the top, C.J. One, two, three."

This time she waited until the last number was uttered, then bore down as hard as she could, pushing with all her strength.

She thought her eyes were going to pop out of her head when she heard him yelling at her.

"Stop, stop."

Gasping, C.J. fell back on the floor again. She was sucking in air, and her head was spinning badly. She was afraid she was going to pass out at any moment, and struggled to hold on to the world around her.

"It's...not...working...is...it?"

How many times did it take to push out a baby? he wondered. One look at C.J. told him that she couldn't take very much more of this.

He took it one step at a time. And lied. "One more time."

But she knew better. He could fool everyone else, but not her.

"You're...lying." Tears and sweat were mingling in her eyes, sliding down her cheeks, pooling beneath her back. "I...can't do...this...Warrick. I'm...not...cut out...for...this...kind of thing." Each word felt like a boulder she was trying to push up a hill.

There was no giving up now. He couldn't let her. "Yes, you are." His voice was fierce. "You're the toughest woman I know. Now c'mon, one more time." Abandoning his post at her nether end, he brought his face up close to hers and implored, "C.J., one more time. Just one more time."

Damn it, why didn't he just let her die? "I…hate…to see you…beg." With superhuman strength, she drew her elbows in to her sides and pushed herself up again. Her head was spinning worse than a top that was out of control. "Okay…let's get…this watermelon…out…of me!"

Warrick strengthened his resolve. "Let's get serious now. Ready, C.J.?"

She wasn't ready, would probably never be ready again. Probably would never be able to breathe right again, either. But there was no postponing this and coming back tomorrow, refreshed and braced. She was in all the way.

It was now or never.

Sucking in one more breath to fortify her, she nodded at Warrick. C.J. screwed her eyes shut and bore down with every last fiber in her body. It felt like forever. She could swear she felt her blood boiling in her veins.

An eternity later C.J. fell back against the floor, hardly aware of what she was doing. Only aware that there was some kind of noise buzzing in her head. No, outside her head. A wailing sound that could have been coming from somewhere else. Or maybe even from her. She wasn't sure.

Wonder was filtering through him. He was supporting an infant's head in the palm of his hand. The emotion was almost indescribable. Warrick looked up at C.J. For a second it looked as if she wasn't moving. "C.J., don't pass out on me now, you're almost finished."

A lot he knew. She had no idea where the strength came from to form the words. "I...*am*... finished."

"No, a little more," he coaxed, infinitely grateful that God hadn't made him a woman. There was no way he could have gone through this, he thought. "You have to push out the baby's shoulders."

There was no energy left to breathe, much less to push. "Can't...you...just...pull?"

"C.J., push," he ordered.

Swirling through her head was the vague thought that she was going to hold Sherry and Joanna accountable for not telling her that giving birth was like trying to expel a giant bowling ball through her nose and that everything inside her body felt as if it was being ripped apart by a pair of giant hands.

"C.J., you have to push!"

She had to die was what she had to do, C.J. thought in despair. No, a faraway voice echoed in her head, the baby, the baby needs you. Your baby. You can't quit now.

"Now!"

Hating Warrick, C.J. propped herself up one last time. She knew in her heart that if the baby didn't completely come out with this effort, she was going to die this way, midpush.

She glared at Warrick. "Count," she gasped angrily.

If looks could kill, he'd be dead right now, Warrick thought. "One—two—three. Push!"

Glancing at her face just before he gave the command, Warrick saw the sweat pouring down into her eyes, saw the look of complete exhaustion on her face. If he could have, he would have changed places with her.

Just like he would have been willing to take a bullet for her any day of the week. She was his partner, his friend, and the person who knew him better than anyone, warts and all. He cared about her more than he cared about anyone else in the world.

The next moment, he was holding her daughter in his hands.

The wailing increased. Was something wrong? Was there something wrong with her baby? *Oh, please let the baby be all right.* C.J. was lying in a heap on the floor. There wasn't a single part of her that didn't ache and wasn't all but smothered in utter exhaustion. It took all she had to raise her head.

"What—"

He grinned, making sure the baby's passageways were all clear. That much he remembered from his training. She was breathing. The life he held against his chest was breathing. He couldn't describe the feeling going on *in* his chest. "A girl."

A girl. She had a daughter. She felt like crying. "What…what does she…look like?"

"A guppy in Jell-O. A beautiful guppy," he qualified, looking up at C.J.

Something very strange was going on inside of him. There was relief because it was over and because C.J. was still alive. He could afford to admit to himself now that he had been laboring under the very real fear that something could have gone wrong during the childbirth. Something could *always* go wrong.

But there was also something else, another feeling that he couldn't readily identify. Something he was unfamiliar with.

It felt as if there were suddenly a rainbow inside of him. A rainbow that seemed to be also raining sunshine.

Quickly he did a tally of the baby's fingers and toes. All were accounted for. He looked up at C.J. "Want to see her?"

She barely had enough strength to form the word. "Please."

Holding the moments-old infant against him, Warrick moved on his knees until he was level with C.J.'s face. But as he began to transfer the baby into her arms, he looked down at the small face. The infant had ceased crying and was simply looking up at him, her eyes as wide as spring flowers sunning themselves.

He felt as if she was looking right into him, right into his heart. Which only seemed fair since it was already hers.

"This is your mother," he whispered to the infant. "Be kind, honey, she's still a work in progress."

He was surprised the words came out at all. It felt as if his throat was constricting. For all the different experiences he had gone through in his life, he had never had a moment quite like this before and he wasn't altogether sure what to make of it.

Amid the waves of exhaustion washing over C.J. was a sense of elation. It spread out, covering her completely as Warrick tucked the baby into her arms.

She was here, C.J. thought, her baby was finally here. Her impatience, her fears, everything she'd lived with all these months were fading into the mists as if they hadn't really existed.

Without a hand to wipe them away, C.J. blinked back her tears.

Her baby was finally here.

"Hi, baby," she said softly to the infant warming her breast. "That was just Warrick. Don't let him scare you." And then she raised her eyes to her partner's face. There really were no words that seemed adequate enough. "Thank you."

He grinned, rocking back on his heels. "It's not as if the two of you left me much choice."

The two of them. It had a nice ring to it, C.J. thought.

Her heart swelling, she tightened her arms around the baby.

Chapter 4

The paramedics arrived ten minutes after he called them.

It occurred to Warrick, as he rode down in the elevator with C.J., the baby and the attendants, that had he gotten on the phone and dialed 911 to begin with, he would have been spared all the trauma he'd just gone through.

And missed out on what was probably the greatest experience of his life.

He smiled to himself as they all got out and he hurried behind the gurney. It made him glad that for once he had been slow to follow through on his original instincts.

Warrick stepped out of the way to allow the paramedics to slide C.J.'s gurney into the ambulance. At that moment, as he watched, she looked very vulnerable. It placed her in an entirely new light for him. She'd probably punch him out if she knew what he was thinking, he thought. But that didn't change the fact that he had an overwhelming desire to be there for her, to somehow shield her, although from what he hadn't the vaguest idea.

Had to be the high he was still running on because of the delivery, he decided.

With the gurney secured in place, Warrick started to climb into the ambulance.

The paramedic beside C.J. placed a hand out to block his entrance. "Only relatives ride in the back with the patient." He cocked his head, scrutinizing him. "You her husband, buddy?"

"That's Special Agent Buddy," C.J. informed him. "And he's my partner."

Unconvinced as to the propriety of all this, the attendant raised his brow. "Like a life partner?"

Warrick glanced toward C.J. and saw that she was looking at him, amusement highlighting her exhausted features. That she could smile after what she'd just been through amazed him.

"Maybe as in life sentence," he cracked. "We work together."

That settled it for the attendant. He reached for the doors, ready to pull them shut. "Sorry, then you've got to follow behind in your car."

Warrick was quick to get his hand up, blocking the doors before they closed. He looked at C.J. Hers was the only opinion that mattered in this. "You want me in the ambulance?"

Under normal circumstances, her answer would

have been flippant. But these weren't normal circumstances. She was feeling elated and teary and a hundred other things. She needed someone there with her to run interference until she could pull herself together. "Yes."

Warrick looked meaningfully at the paramedic. "Then, it's settled."

The paramedic raised his hands, surrendering and backing off. "Sorry, just stating company policy, Special Agent."

"I'll take it up with your boss," Warrick said, climbing on.

The trip to Blair Memorial Hospital took just long enough for Warrick to make the necessary call to her parents. He left it up to Diane to notify the others, knowing it would probably take a matter of seconds.

He was right. C.J.'s family converged on the hospital less than ten minutes after the front desk had found a room for her on the maternity floor.

The six-foot-two nurse with the kindly smile had no sooner helped C.J. slip into bed than Warrick was knocking on the door. He peered into the room just as she said, "Come in."

Some of C.J.'s color was returning, he noted. She was beginning to look like her old self again. Feisty and contrary. He felt relieved. "Got some people out here who for reasons beyond me seem to be awfully anxious to see you. Can they come in?"

As independent of ties as she liked to pretend to be, C.J. had to admit that it felt good to know that she had family close by who cared about her. "I guess we can't keep them out, can we?"

"You just try, sweetheart," her father said, pushing past Warrick as he sailed into the room. Nodding at the nurse who was a shade taller than he was, James Jones elbowed his way next to the bed and took one of his daughter's hands into both of his. His blue eyes crinkled, barely disguising the concern etched on his face. "How are you, darlin'?"

"Tired." C.J. tried to rally, summoning what energy she could. Her brothers surrounded her bed, leaving a space for her mother directly opposite her father. "How did you all manage to get here so fast?"

"Dad broke a few speed limits," Diane told her, attempting to look annoyed but not quite pulling it off. "What are you doing, having this baby without me? I thought I was supposed to be your coach."

C.J. glanced at Warrick who was standing at the foot of her bed behind one of her brothers. "I had to settle for second best."

Diane turned her attention to the man she had taken aside and charged with her daughter's care the very first time she'd met him. "Thank God you were there to help her, Byron."

C.J.'s eyes shifted toward her partner. As ever, the use of his given name didn't seem to faze him when her mother called him by it. It still amazed her. She supposed he more or less considered her family to be his own. Her brothers were his friends, and her mother and father were like a second set of parents to him.

Or maybe even a first set from the little she'd managed to get out of him about his childhood. Warrick had been an only child. An accident of nature was the way he had put it once. His parents had kept him, much the way a customer keeps an item they'd accidentally broken in a shop and were forced to pay for. The relationship was that sterile.

There was no mention of love, of affection existing in his past, even remotely. He rarely spoke about them, even when she asked him direct questions. His father had died some years back and his mother had remarried and was living out of the country. Even that had not come firsthand to her. Warrick had told her mother one rainy Sunday afternoon after watching a football game on TV with the male contingent of her family.

It amazed C.J. how much information her mother could get out of her closemouthed partner. There were times when she honestly thought her mother had missed her calling, although, to hear Diane Jones tell it, being the wife of a prominent criminal lawyer and the mother of three more, plus another potential up-and-coming barrister as well as an FBI agent, was more than satisfying enough for her.

That her mother added her as an addendum was just a trademark of her sense of humor. C.J. knew that her mother doted so much on her that it was difficult for the woman not to show it.

Warrick shrugged carelessly at her mother's comment. "C.J. did most of the work."

"*Most* of it?" C.J. hooted. "Ha! I did all of it."

"Knowing C.J., you're lucky to have come out

of the ordeal alive," Brian, her oldest brother, said to Warrick.

Warrick poked his tongue into his cheek. "She did get a little testy."

"Spoken like a typical man," C.J. countered. "You try pushing out an elephant through a keyhole, see how cheerful you stay."

Ever the referee even after her children were grown, Diane held up her hands, waving all involved parties into silence.

"Enough. The bottom line is that the baby's here, Chris is all right, and we're all together." She laced her arm through her husband's, glowing with contentment. "So, have you decided what my new granddaughter's name is?"

C.J. shook her head. Ever mindful of the possibility that something might go wrong, she had refused to think of any names for either sex while she was pregnant. "No, not yet."

Her father looked at her, his disappointment apparent. "Not even one name? Oh, Christmas, you even put that off?"

C.J. shut her eyes. Christmas Morgan were her official given names, laid on her by an act of whimsy on her father's part because she'd been born on Christmas morning.

When she opened her eyes again, it was to look at the guilty party. "Well, when I do come up with a name, it's going to be a hell of a lot better than 'Christmas,' I can promise you that."

Warrick grinned. He knew this was a really sensitive topic for her. "What's the matter with being called Christmas? Although I have to admit, it doesn't exactly suit you."

"And just exactly what is that supposed to mean?" she wanted to know.

Ethan nudged Jamie, the baby of the family. "Nice to see that the miracle of birth hasn't changed you any, Chris."

She was feeling better already. Having her family here was the best medicine of all. "Maybe growing up in a houseful of boys had something to do with that," she pointed out. "I had to be twice as good as each of you just to hold my own."

"Your own what?" Jamie cracked. As the youngest, he was forever struggling to find his own place in a family of overachievers. The fact that at six-five, he towered over all of them helped to help balance things out.

"Her own everything," Wayne said. With two brothers born before him and a sister and brother born after, Wayne was the most even tempered of the family, given to thinking twice before speaking once. It was a trait his mother often wished out loud had been spread out amid her other children. Moving forward, Wayne brushed a kiss on his sister's forehead. "Get some rest, kid. You look like hell."

"Thanks." Her eyes met her brother's. "You always did know what to say to perk a girl right up."

"Why don't we all leave and let Chris get some well-deserved rest?" Diane suggested.

"Which way's the nursery?" Brian wanted to know.

"Can we see the baby?" Ethan chimed in.

"Do they have her in an incubator?" Jamie wanted to know.

"No." C.J. finally managed to get in a word. "She weighed in just over five pounds. The doctor said she's strong and healthy.

"Of course she is," her father said. "She's my granddaughter."

"Yes, dear," Diane patted his face. "You deserve all the credit here." Turning her head, she winked at her daughter.

One by one her family filed by, kissing her and taking their leave. Diane waited for them at the door, making sure her brood made it into the hallway. But when Warrick moved to follow, she shook her head.

"Why don't you stick around a little while longer, Byron? She might like the company. Maybe even get around to apologizing for being so testy with you earlier as you put it."

Warrick glanced over his shoulder toward C.J. She nodded. "Okay, just for a few more minutes."

Diane paused at the door, the men in her life waiting for her to join them in the hall. Placing a hand on Warrick's shoulder, she raised herself up on her toes and brushed her lips against his cheek. "Thank you for being there for her."

His smile was almost shy. "Just a matter of being in the right place at the right time."

"I'm glad it was you." She turned toward her daughter, beaming. Her baby had had a baby. "You did good, honey. I'll see you in the morning. And don't forget, think of some names."

C.J. nodded. Warrick let the door close and then crossed to her. "You really don't have any names?"

She shrugged her shoulders. The hospital gown slipped off one, and she tugged it back into place. "Not a one."

He shook his head. She had been damned determined not to allow her pregnancy to interfere with her work. No one knew until it was absolutely necessary. The only reason he'd found out before the others was because he'd stumbled onto her condition completely by accident. While on a stakeout, she would periodically bolt out of the car and dash for the closest bathroom. It didn't take him long to figure out she wasn't battling food poisoning but morning sickness.

Warrick leaned against the wall, studying her. "Never knew you to be this unprepared before, Jones."

She offered him a wan smile, her mind half a world away. This was supposed to have been a happy time. Instead she'd just joined the ranks of single motherhood with all its scary ramifications. Served her right for veering from her course and thinking that maybe she'd been one of the lucky ones to find someone special. What had led her down this primrose path was that her parents seemed so happy together. It had made her believe that marriages, if not made in heaven, certainly created one of their own. Well, Thorndyke had certainly set her straight about that.

"Some things," she murmured, "you're never prepared for."

Something inside of his gut tightened. He knew she was thinking about Thorndyke. Warrick could feel his blood pressure going up several notches at the very thought of the man and his emotional abandonment of C.J. This time he kept his comment to himself. She'd been through hell, and he didn't want to agitate her right now with any negative comments about the poster boy for slime. Thorndyke had obviously made her happy once and whatever did that was okay with him.

At least, he tried to tell himself that, although how she could be happy, even for a moment, with that shallow pretty boy was beyond him. If he didn't know better, he would have said he was experiencing a bout of jealousy. But he did know better.

Rather than use the chair beside her, Warrick sat down on the bed and looked at C.J. for a long moment. That strange, funny feeling he'd gotten the moment he'd held her daughter in his hands hadn't completely dissipated. On the contrary, alone with C.J. like this, it seemed to take on more depth and breadth. He still couldn't put a name to it. Maybe it was better that way.

He looked at her pointedly. "He should know."

She'd expected another put-down of her ex-lover. She certainly didn't think Warrick was going to push for any sort of contact. C.J. raised her chin defensively. "He knows."

"You called him?" There hadn't been any time, unless she'd done it while he was filling out her insurance papers at the registration desk.

C.J. looked away, in no mood for a lecture. "I

told him I was pregnant, A baby is usually the end result of that condition.''

Cupping her face, he made her look at him. ''You weren't that sure,'' he reminded her.

She pulled her head back. So he was Tom's champion now? ''I don't count.''

A very soft smile curved Warrick's mouth as he said quietly, ''Yes, you do.'' And then he straightened. ''Thorndyke doesn't know he has a daughter.''

Their last conversation together, the one that was littered with words like, ''no strings'' and ''hey, how I do I know it's even mine?'' played itself over in her head. She'd hated Thorndyke for that, hated him for making what they'd shared seem tawdry and cheap. The one time she'd let her guard down and it had to be with the wrong man.

And now her partner was just making things worse. ''He doesn't *want* to know.'' She raised her voice. ''Will you leave it alone, Warrick? He's like you. No strings.''

Warrick's brows narrowed over stormy eyes. There was no way he'd allow himself to be compared to the other man. ''He's *not* like me. I'd want to know. I wouldn't have left you to begin with.''

The tightly reined-in emotion in his voice surprised her. ''You didn't,'' she told him.

He'd almost lost it just then. Maybe this whole baby thing had him more wound up than he thought. Warrick cleared his throat. ''Yeah, I know. Do you want me to find him?''

Did he really think she didn't know where her baby's father was? "No need."

Warrick looked into her eyes. He was the detail person and she was the one who went in like gangbusters, but it was stupid of him to think for a second that she wouldn't keep tabs on Thorndyke, if only to make sure there was space between them.

"You know where he is, don't you?"

"He's in D.C.," she told him crisply, and then added, "And if you get in contact with him in any way, I'll rip your heart out."

He laughed softly, letting the matter go. After all, it was her life. And maybe he was even a little relieved that she *didn't* want to see Thorndyke, though there was no way he would ever have admitted to that.

"Always the delicate lady."

A little of the luster returned to her eyes. "And don't you forget it." There had been only one detail about her pregnancy that she'd planned. "Now, are you going to be the baby's godfather?"

The request, coming out of the blue, almost rendered him speechless. It took him a second to recover. "I'd be honored."

She shrugged, trying not to let him see how much it meant to her to have him agree to be her baby's godfather. "Just be there. Otherwise I'd have to substitute one of my brothers and that's like putting a double whammy on the baby. Grossly unfair."

"Wouldn't want that." He rose. It was time to go. There were only five hours until morning. "So, you want me to draw up a list for you?"

The question caught her off guard. She thought of the case she'd been poring over when this had all started. "Of suspects?"

"Of possible names." She was unbelievable. "Damn it, C.J., you just gave birth. How can you be thinking about serial killers at a time like this?"

He didn't understand, did he? Now it was personal. "*Because* I just gave birth to a little girl not unlike thirteen other little girls, that's why I can be thinking about bringing this scum in. Each one of these thirteen victims had a first day, Warrick, just like my baby. Each one of them was someone's little girl."

He understood where she was coming from, but he was shooting for something far less complex. Leaning over her bed, he tucked the blanket up around her waist. "Stop being an FBI agent for a few minutes, C.J. Just for tonight, be little what's-its-name's mom."

He had no idea what she was experiencing, C.J. thought. How hard it was to keep the tears from forming in her eyes. Maybe it was just her hormones, running amok, but she was filled with so much love, so much *everything* that it was a miracle she was even able to draw a breath in. It felt so crowded inside of her.

But there was no way anyone, not even Warrick, was ever going to see just how vulnerable she actually could be. Weakness was always exploited, intentionally or otherwise.

"Okay," she finally allowed somewhat cavalierly. "But promise me you'll keep me posted about the case."

"Right." There was no way one word about the case was going to reach her ears from his lips until she was back to active duty, he thought, smiling at her. "I'll call if there's any breakthrough."

That was too easy. She knew him better than that. "I'm not kidding."

"I know." Warrick took her hands into his and looked into her eyes, his expression softening just a little. Until a few hours ago he would have said that he was as close to C.J. as he was ever going to get. He'd been wrong.

Maybe it was just the excess of emotions he was feeling, he thought, searching for a reason for what was going on inside of him. "Don't you ever relax?"

C.J. pressed her lips together. "The last time I relaxed, I wound up pregnant." She instantly regretted the confession, but as she watched his eyes, she realized with relief that Warrick was being sympathetic.

He shook his head. "I know this is a new concept for you, Jones, but try for middle ground." He bent over the bed, intending to brush a kiss on her cheek. Caught off guard, she turned her head. Her lips made contact with his. It was hard to say who was more surprised.

Something that had all the markings of an electric current snaked its way through her at lightning speed, making every hair on her body stand on end. She knew it was only a matter of extreme exhaustion mingled with being emotionally overwrought, but the end effect was still the same.

Her heart was pounding almost as hard as it had when she was struggling to give birth.

Very slowly Warrick lifted his head. His eyes held hers for a beat before he took a step back. He was as unsure of what had just transpired here as he had been about the feeling that had taken hold of him in the field office.

"You missed your target entirely," she said quietly, struggling for a fragment of composure. She felt as if she was going to shatter into a million pieces if he so much as blew in her direction. "I think you'd better get back on the firing range."

Warrick laughed then and ran his thumb along her bottom lip, wiping off the imprint of his lips. "Don't worry about my ability to shoot straight. I can handle my own. See you tomorrow, Mommy."

That term was reserved for her daughter when she learned to talk. C.J. loathed couples who referred to one another that way. "Don't call me that."

He paused. "'Daddy' doesn't seem to fit, even if you do wear the pants most of the time."

She didn't want him thinking of her any differently. Not because of the baby. And not because of what had just accidentally happened here. "I'm still C.J.," she insisted.

"Yeah," he agreed. His eyes swept over her. "You're still C.J. But as of two hours ago, you're now a hell of a lot more."

He winked at her and left.

Chapter 5

That old familiar feeling came over her. The one where she felt as if she was in the right place, where she was meant to be.

After completing three weeks of her maternity leave, C.J. absorbed her surroundings as she made her way from the elevator and down the hall. The last time she'd been here, she'd been done in by exhaustion, flat on her back and strapped to a gurney on the way to the hospital with a minutes-old baby in her arms.

God it felt good to be back.

She took a moment to gather herself together outside the office she shared with Rodriguez, Culpepper and Warrick, then pushed open the door.

Culpepper was the first to see her. Portly, with a

layer of muscle beneath the fat, he rose to his feet and came forward.

"Hey, looks who's here, Rodriguez. How's it going, Mommy?"

Tossing her purse on her desk, she glanced toward her partner. "Warrick, did you warn these people about calling me that?"

"Hey, I can't help it if they all have the attention spans of baby gnats." Their desks butted up against each other. He rounded his and came to stand by hers. "Speaking of baby, why aren't you with yours?"

She took a deep breath. Slightly stale air, lemon floor polish and Rodriguez's ever-present jar of peanut butter. It even smelled good to be back here.

"The doctor gave me a clean bill of health, said I was fit to report back for duty." C.J. had left the appropriate papers down at personnel on her way up here. "She actually thought I would be a nicer person if I went off to work every day."

That was because even despite the work a new baby required, C.J. found herself going stir-crazy. The ability to multitask with speed was not always a good thing. It left her with too much time on her hands. She needed to fill that time with her job. Besides, ever since she'd become a mother herself, she had this overwhelming need to make the world around her a safer place to be for her daughter. She was doing it the only way she knew how.

"Besides," C.J. continued, "My daughter's actually got the semblance of a sleeping schedule down, and I've been kept in the dark long enough."

She looked at Warrick pointedly, then turned her attention to the other two men who were part of the Sleeping Beauty Killer's task force. "Can either one of you two fill me in?" She nodded toward Warrick. "My partner here refused to say a word about the case to me. Every time I asked, he kept changing the subject so much, I began thinking that maybe Warrick was the Artful Dodger come to life."

"Artful anything doesn't sound like Warrick," Ralph Culpepper hooted.

"Never mind that." She sat down at the edge of her seat, as if poised to leap up at any second, Warrick noticed. Same old C.J. "I need input," she told them. "Someone brief me."

George Rodriguez raised and lowered his wide shoulders. At six-five, everything he did was big. "Nothing to brief, C.J., our boy's laying low again. Maybe we'll get lucky and it'll be another three-year reprieve."

That wasn't the way she saw it. "We'll get lucky when we nail the son of a bitch." As long as the serial killer wasn't off the streets, he could always strike again. "So nothing's been happening while I've been out of touch?" C.J. underscored the final word, sending an accusing glance Warrick's way.

"Well, Rodriguez, here, got engaged." Culpepper slapped his partner on the back. Sitting, Rodriguez was almost as tall as Culpepper was standing.

She hadn't even known he was seeing anyone. "Is that true?" Squirming ever so slightly in his seat, Rodriguez nodded. "Who is she?"

Culpepper answered for him. A new grandfather,

he looked upon his partner as a son. He was accustomed to doing most of the talking. "You know that cute little receptionist on the second floor?"

C.J. thought a minute. Her eyes widened as she realized who Culpepper was talking about. "You mean that little-bitty dark-haired one who looks like she wears size-one clothes?"

Culpepper grinned at Rodriguez, who was taking a considerable interest in the file he was holding open in his hands. "That's the one."

Talk about the long and the short of it. "What are you going to do, Rodriguez," C.J. asked, "carry her around in your pocket?"

"For starters," Culpepper laughed, nudging his partner and winking broadly.

Rodriguez had only been at the Bureau for three and a half years. She still thought of him as "the new guy." "Well, I'm very happy for you, Rodriguez. Don't forget to let me know when the wedding is."

Culpepper sat down and leaned back in his chair. "Hey, talking about weddings, I hear there's a rash of those going on. Any of you remember Tom Thorndyke, that tall dude who used to work down the hall?" He looked from Warrick to his partner and then at C.J. "You went out with him, didn't you C.J.?"

Damn it, why did her heart just skip a beat? She thought she'd drummed that bastard out of her system. "Once or twice," she allowed. She congratulated herself for keeping her smile in place. "What about him?"

Warrick slanted a look at C.J. There was no way he could prevent the conversation from continuing without alerting the other two men that something was wrong. No one else knew that the absent special agent was the father of C.J.'s baby.

Culpepper's chair creaked. "Word is he's getting married."

"Married?" The word tasted like dried cardboard in her mouth. She struggled to sound only mildly interested. Anger mingled with surprise. "Really? To who?"

Culpepper scrubbed his hand over his face, thinking. He prided himself on always getting his facts right. "Somebody he met while on the job. One of the bean counters." Every organization had them. Even the Bureau. "She moved out with him when he transferred. Got the story from the guy who used to be his partner." He glanced at C.J. "All these weddings, must be something in the water, eh, C.J.?"

"Must be."

She knew that Culpepper wasn't trying to be insensitive. The oldest of them by twenty years, it was probably his fatherly way of suggesting that she herself find someone to marry, to give her baby a proper father. He had no way of knowing that he'd struck a bad chord.

Picking up her purse, she pretended to look through it. "I think I left something back in the car." Dropping the purse, she rose to her feet, keys in hand. "I'll be right back."

"Pictures of the baby, I'll bet," Culpepper chuckled. He looked at Rodriguez. "They've always got pictures."

Warrick hurried after C.J. She'd managed to get far ahead of him in the hall. He lengthened his stride.

"Hey, Jones, wait up. Didn't the doctor tell you not to start jogging the same day you went back to work?" Catching up to her, he took hold of her arm, bringing her to a halt. "C'mon, C.J., stop for a minute and talk to me."

She didn't want to talk to anybody. She wanted to kick something, break something. Vent. But because Warrick had placed himself in the line of fire, she took it out on him.

"Did you know?" she demanded.

He didn't know if she was hurt or about to spit fire. With C.J. it was hard to tell. "I—"

Her eyes narrowed accusingly. "Did you know?"

He made it a point not to lie. Especially not to a friend. The closest he came was to omit mentioning things. But there was no space for that here.

Warrick threw his hands up. "Hell, C.J. what do you want me to tell you? Yes, I knew. I heard via the grapevine last week just like blabbermouth in there." He silently cursed Culpepper. Why couldn't the man have been out of the office when she came back?

"And you didn't tell me." How could he? she demanded silently. How could he have known and not told her?

"Why should I?" He hadn't told her because he didn't want to reopen any wounds that might have been healing. "You said you moved on, remember? You told me in the hospital that you didn't want to get in contact with him—ever."

"I didn't. I don't." Confusion was running riot through her. She honestly thought she was over the man. But if so, why this sudden onslaught of pain? What the hell was wrong with her? "It's just that..." Anger creased her brow as she looked up at him. "Damn it, War, here I thought he didn't want to get involved and it was that he just didn't want to get involved with me." And being rejected stung. "I guess it just hurts my pride, that's all."

He bracketed her shoulders with his hands. Wanting to protect her. Knowing she'd bite off his head if he even hinted at it. "Just goes to prove how stupid the guy really was, letting someone like you go. Look, I didn't tell you because I didn't want you reacting this way. He's not worth it, C.J. You know it, I know it. End of story."

"Yeah, end of story," she echoed, then thought of her daughter and how hard it had been to leave her this morning. She'd never known she could fall in love so completely and with such little effort. But she had. And if not for Thorndyke, Joy wouldn't have existed. And all that love C.J. felt within her at this moment wouldn't have even materialized. "I guess I got the best part of him anyway."

He'd been out in the field for the last week and hadn't had time to drop by to visit C.J. "Speaking of which, how's my future goddaughter doing?"

C.J. thought of the way she felt walking to her

car after dropping the infant off. Empty, as if a part of her was suddenly missing.

"A lot better than me. I left her the center of attention at my mother's house." She'd never realized just how much her mother had wanted to be a grandmother. "My parents have more baby furniture and toys for Joy than I do." This despite the impromptu shower the Mom Squad had thrown her when she'd come home from the hospital.

He saw nothing surprising about that. "Why not? They had five kids—and an attic." He crossed his arms before his chest. "So I take it she didn't have any—what do they call it?—separation anxiety?"

C.J. laughed shortly. "She didn't. I did." Even now she couldn't help wondering what her baby was doing. Did she realize C.J. wasn't around? Or was Mommy just another face to look up at? God, but she was getting mushy. How long before hormones adjusted themselves back into place? And then she looked at Warrick in wonder. "How do you know about separation anxiety, anyway?"

He was the methodical one. "I thought that since I'm supposed to be her godfather, I should bone up on these things." He looked at his partner pointedly. "I should also insist that she have a middle name to go with the first name. You can't just call her Joy Jones."

She saw nothing wrong with that. "Why not?"

"Do you want people to call her 'J.J.'?"

"I don't just want her to have any old middle name. I want the whole name to be special. To fit her."

Time was running out, Warrick thought. The christening was set for next week. "Okay, what d'you say I come over tonight after work with a book of baby names, and we'll start tossing out names at her? One of them is bound to stick."

"Sounds like a plan."

He cocked his head and peered at her, the teasing note gone from his voice. "You going to be okay?"

She tossed her hair over her shoulder, raising her chin. He was familiar with that move. It was her "the world can go to hell" gesture. "I'm already okay. Just took the wind out of my sails, that's all. Worse things could have happened, right?"

"Right. You could be marrying the guy." They began to walk back down the hall when he stopped her again. "Hey, have you got any pictures of the baby with you?"

She thought that was an odd question, coming from him. "In my purse. Brian's been snapping his camera so much around her, she's probably debating getting a career as a model right now. Why?"

"Because Culpepper's expecting you to come back with pictures." He didn't want the other man quizzing her and having his suspicions raised. Culpepper might come off as a busybody, but there was nothing wrong with his deductive reasoning. "He thinks that's what you went to get from your car."

"I'll just tell him I made a mistake." But as they started to walk again, she placed a hand on his arm. She had to ask. "War, does anyone else know? About Thorndyke and me?"

Warrick shook his head. "Not unless Thorndyke

told them, and considering how fast he put in for a transfer to another field office after you told him, I really don't think he did.''

"Good." Despite the fact that she was outgoing, C.J. hated having her business plastered all over the office.

She supposed that gave her something in common with Warrick.

"It was good to go back to work, but it's even better to come back to you," C.J. told her baby as she let herself into her house. "I forgot how long days could feel.''

Still holding Joy in her infant seat, C.J. kicked off her shoes and wiggled her toes. The rug felt good beneath her feet.

Despite her mother's protests and her offer to make dinner, C.J. had opted to come home to snare a little peace and quiet, or a reasonable facsimile thereof. The day had been deadly dull and overly long, at least it seemed that way. Their investigation was going nowhere—slowly. At times it felt as if every minute was being individually held hostage, doubling in size before it was released.

She supposed that missing her daughter had something to do with that. At twenty-eight, she was surprised to find out something new about herself.

C.J. rotated her neck, trying to ease away some of the tension. She looked down into the car seat. Joy's eyes were shut, long black lashes creating dark crescents along her cheeks.

"Oh, honey, are you asleep already? I thought I'd

get in a little quality time with you.'' She banked down her disappointment. ''I guess not.'' She smiled to herself. ''With my luck, you'll probably want quality time at two in the morning.''

Carrying the infant seat over to a safe, flat surface, C.J. placed it on the dining room table. Careful not to wake the baby, she unbuckled the restraining straps one at a time.

''Well, don't get used to being a dictator. Once you figure this language of ours out and can understand me, there are going to be lines to toe, young lady, and hoops to jump through.'' She laughed, nuzzling her daughter as she picked her up out of the infant seat. ''Yeah, and I'll probably be the one doing the toeing and the leaping. Just don't tell anyone your mom's a softie, okay? It'll be our little secret.''

Holding her daughter in the crook of her arm, C.J. looked down at the perfect little face. ''Slept right through that, didn't you? Next you'll be telling me I'm boring.'' She thought of the news about Thorndyke and his wedding. ''Maybe I am at that. Okay, enough pity. Let's get you into bed, my love.''

The baby made no protest.

After making sure the baby monitor, with its multiple receiving units that she'd placed in each room, was turned on, C.J. gently closed the nursery door.

The doorbell rang.

She sighed. Now what?

Training had her glancing at her holstered gun on the hall table before approaching the front door. The weapon was in easy reach, just in case. "Who is it?" she called out.

"Rumpelstiltskin. Who do you think? Open the door, C.J."

Warrick. Their conversation in the hallway came back to her. She'd completely forgotten.

About to appeal to his better nature and beg off, C.J. opened the door She didn't get the opportunity to say the words. Warrick walked in, juggling a large pizza box in one hand and a couple of books in the other. He held the latter aloft.

"I come bearing pizza and not *one* baby name book, but two." He tossed the books on the sofa as he came into the living room. "I couldn't decide between the two and thought I'd splurge. I figured, Murphy's Law, the one I didn't buy would have the name that appealed to you." The coffee table was littered with papers. She was the only one he knew who was a worse housekeeper than he was. "Where do you want this?" He indicated the pizza. "It's hot."

Walking ahead of him, she moved the infant seat off the table and put it on the floor in the corner. "You didn't have to bring that."

He was already opening the box. The smell of pepperoni and three kinds of cheeses filled the air. "Hey, I've got to eat, too."

C.J. went to the kitchen and reached into the cupboard for a couple of plates. "I could always have rustled up something."

He shivered at the thought. "No offense but I'd rather eat my shoes." He took a plate from her.

"You're a woman of many talents, C.J. Cooking is not one of them." He held up the first slice, offering it to her. "My dog cooks better than you."

She slid the slice onto her plate and sat down at the table. "You don't have a dog."

He took a slice for himself. "If I did, he'd cook better than you." He sank his teeth into the slice and savored the taste. It had taken him almost four years to find the right pizza place. It wasn't just about tossing the right ingredients onto dough, it was about care and timing and crust. Though his body gave no indication of it, Warrick loved his food. "And I'm thinking about getting one."

She stopped midbite. "You?"

He could just hear her mocking him. "Is that so hard to imagine?"

"Yes. I can't see you getting attached to anything." His marriage and its disastrous termination testified to that.

"Who says I'm the one getting attached? Dogs are supposed to be the loyal ones, the ones that stand by the door, waiting for you to come home." He had to admit, he kind of liked the thought of having something there to greet him. Though he enjoyed his solitude, there were times when there was too much of it.

"Good luck with that." She took another bite, then looked at him. "And since when do you care about those kinds of things, anyway?"

He wasn't about to admit to having a real need. "Seems like the right thing to do. Then my goddaughter would have something to play with whenever she came over to visit.''

''My daughter's coming over to your house? When did this happen?''

''Well, not right now.'' Polishing off the slice, he helped himself to another. ''I mean later. When she can walk and talk and stuff. I haven't even got the dog yet,'' he pointed out.

C.J. laughed and shook her head. Getting up, she went to get a couple of napkins.

''If you ask me, I came back from maternity leave just in time.'' She tossed several napkins on the table between them. ''You sound like you're losing your mind.''

He had to admit he'd missed having her around. ''Rodriguez and Culpepper aren't exactly next week's contestants for Jeopardy.'' At least not as far as day-to-day conversations went. ''All Culpepper wants to talk about is that gopher he's been battling since the beginning of time, and Rodriguez keeps getting that goofy look on his face whenever he thinks about his fiancée.''

''How can you tell the difference? He always looks goofy.''

Warrick laughed. ''Goofier.'' He realized he needed something to drink. ''I didn't bring beer, I didn't know if you were, um, you know.''

''No, I'm not, um, you know.'' Getting up, she went to the refrigerator and fetched a bottle of beer for him and a can of diet soda for herself. ''The baby's pediatrician said she needs a special formula. Seems that she's allergic—''

Warrick held up his hand. "Too much information." He felt this was getting into a realm he had no business being in. "That's violating doctor-patient privilege."

"How much privilege are we talking about?" C.J. laughed, then looked at her partner. Was that a pink hue she saw creeping up his cheek? Warrick? This was a man who'd busted a prostitution ring and walked in on two naked women without blinking an eye. "Pink is not your color, Warrick."

He pushed the box toward her. "Why don't you just finish eating so we can get down to business?"

She helped herself to a second slice. "Okay, but I warn you," her eyes indicated the books, "this might not work."

"Every known name in the world is in these books. If you can't find a middle name here, you're going to have to make one up."

She hadn't thought of that. The idea was not without its appeal. "There's an idea."

Warrick was sorry he'd said anything. "Let's just leave it on the back burner until we've gone through this."

"Whatever you say."

He gave her a dubious look. "Now there's something I never thought I'd hear from you."

The sound of her laughter enveloped him. He'd missed that, too, Warrick thought as he got up to get the books.

Chapter 6

Warrick shook his head as he got up from the living room sofa. It was getting late and they had more than done justice to the pizza, if not to the quest for a suitable middle name for C.J.'s daughter.

The latter was not for his lack of trying. He glanced at the books on the coffee table. They looked as if they'd been run through the wringer. "You know, you're impossible."

C.J. rose, as well. She stretched before rounding the table to join him.

"No," she said, "I'm selective."

She wasn't any happier about the situation than he sounded, but she was determined not to rush this process. Her daughter's full name had to be absolutely right for her.

Warrick had another word for it, but kept it to himself.

"It's just a middle name. Just pick one."

She glanced back at the books. "I don't know, maybe I went through them too fast, but none of the names I looked at 'feel' right for my daughter." She frowned.

Why did he even bother trying to win an argument with her? "You know, rather than Christmas, your parents should have named you Mary. Like in that nursery rhyme— 'Mary, Mary quite contrary.'" He took a closer look at her. There were shadows beneath her eyes. He hoped her daughter would let her get a few hours rest. "Do you have to disagree with everything I say?"

"I don't have to..." C.J. let her voice trail off. The further it went, the wider her grin became.

Warrick surrendered with a symbolic throwing up of his hands. He had to be getting home. There were a few things he wanted to check into before he went to bed. "You win. I give up."

C.J. picked up the two books he'd brought and held them out to him, but he shook his head.

"You keep these and see if a name does 'feel right' to you." He moved his hands around like a wizard conjuring up a spell.

C.J. put the books back down. "You'll be the first to know," she promised. She walked him to the door and opened it, then lingered a moment in the doorway. "Thanks for the pizza and the books."

He pointed toward them behind her, a headmaster

giving a pupil an assignment. "You've a week, Jones."

She sighed. That did limit her time, she thought. "I know, I know."

"Hey," he leaned his arm on the doorjamb just above her head, "different strokes for different folks. It's what makes the world go around." He moved back a hair that was in her face. Her pupils looked as if they widened just a touch. He felt that same funny stirring in his gut. Again he locked it away. "You're entitled to be a little strange once in a while."

Warrick wasn't sure just what made him do what he did next. He supposed it was a natural by-product of a good evening spent in the company of a good friend, although he'd never brushed a kiss on the cheek of any of the guys he'd interacted with on the basketball court, no matter how good a game had been played.

Whatever the reason behind it, the bottom line was that he leaned over and touched his lips to her cheek, as he'd done in the hospital.

This time it didn't stun her. It didn't even register because just then a cat unleashed a wild screech that sounded as if it was being vivisected somewhere in the vicinity. The unearthly noise startled her, and she jerked, turning her head, just as before.

But this time when their lips met, neither one of them sprang back. Instead they drew together. And allowed the unintentional meeting of two pairs of lips to instantly flower into something a great deal more lethal, a great deal hotter than simply skin against skin.

And a great deal more pleasurable.

He didn't remember doing it. Didn't remember taking hold of C.J.'s shoulders and drawing her up a little higher, a little closer, helping her along as she rose on her toes. Didn't remember deepening the kiss, even though he did.

What he did remember was thinking that now he finally knew what it felt like to be kicked by a mule. Because something sure had found him where he lived and given him a swift, sound kick right to his gut.

Damn, for someone with just a tart tongue, she tasted sweet.

This wasn't happening, it couldn't be happening, she thought. But she was so glad it was.

For one long, everlasting moment, C.J. felt as if her connections to the real world had all been short-circuited and severed. There was no sky above, no ground below, no walls around to contain her. She was free-falling into an abyss, a wild swirling surging in her chest.

Warrick?

This was Warrick?

How the hell could this be Warrick? She'd worked alongside him for more than six years. Possibly, once or twice in an off moment, she'd fantasized what it might be like to be with him in some capacity other than his partner, but nothing that had momentarily traveled through her brain had been remotely close to this.

This was something she didn't know how to begin to describe.

Was that her pulse vibrating so fast? Could he tell? What the hell was happening to her? She was melting all over him.

Limp, she felt limp.

No! No way this was happening to her, not here, not now. Not again.

The next moment, contact was broken. Whether she pushed him back or he'd done it of his own accord, she didn't know. But the sky, the ground and the walls all made a return appearance.

It took all she had to remain standing where she was and not grasp the doorjamb for support.

Very slowly Warrick let out his breath. What he really wanted to do was gulp air in to replenish the lack of it in his lungs and maybe, just maybe, squelch this erratic hammering of his heart.

He looked at her, striving for the nonchalance that was one of the cornerstones of their partnership, hoping his voice didn't give him away. "You've got to learn to stop turning your head at the wrong moment."

She looked at him in surprise. Wrong moment? Did it feel like a wrong moment to him? It felt like a right one to her.

Careful, C.J. you're vulnerable. This is what got you in trouble before. Think, *don't feel.*

She clenched her hands at her sides, pressing her nails into the palms of her hand.

"Maybe if you stop going at my cheek like some hungry chicken pecking at scattered corn, there

wouldn't be any wrong moments.'' One hand
squarely against his chest, she pushed him over the
threshold as she grabbed the door with her other one.
''Thanks for the books, see you tomorrow. Bye.''

Warrick found himself looking at the closed door
before he could utter a single word in response or
defense. Just as well.

He drew in the air he so badly needed, then turned
away and walked to his car on legs that were a little
less solid than they had been when he'd made the
walk to her front door.

C.J. stood leaning against the door, her mind
numb. Which was fine. It went along with the rest
of her body. Numb mind, numb body—it was a set.

Like someone waking up from a dream, not quite
sure what was real and what wasn't, she walked very
slowly to the sofa.

And then collapsed as if every single bone in her
body had just been pulled out.

''You're here already.''

The sound of Warrick's voice behind her had C.J.
straightening slightly. She turned away from one of
several bulletin boards covered with various pieces
of the investigation, determined not to let him suspect that he was partially to blame for her getting
only three hours sleep last night.

''Where else would I be?'' Was it just her, or did
her voice sound a little too high? Where was this
nervousness, this uncertainty coming from? This
was just Warrick, for heaven's sake. A Warrick who
had completely blown her out of the water last night.

She cleared her throat. "We've got a serial killer on the prowl and we're partners on the task force, remember?"

Feeling suddenly awkward, C.J. offered the box of doughnuts she'd stopped to pick up by pushing them toward him on the new appropriated conference table. "Care for a sugar high?"

Warrick made his selection without really looking, then took his prize to the coffeemaker. He'd already had a strong cup of coffee but he felt as if he needed another one. Even stronger this time.

Damn if he could explain why the sight of her alone in the room they had commandeered for their task force made him feel as if he needed to fortify himself somehow.

But it did.

She watched him pick up the mug that had once been white and start pouring. "You know, you really should wash that out once in a while. Bacteria breeds in cleaner places than that. Your mug must seem like Disneyland to them."

"Adds to the taste of the coffee," he muttered. Warrick took his coffee without compromise: black and hot.

She picked up her own half-empty coffee mug, now cooled to the point that it practically looked solid, and stared into it, thinking. The fluorescent lights overhead danced along the surface, adding to the trance.

She blew out a long breath. They could skirt around this, pretend it wasn't there and it would continue to gain depth and breadth, like some white

elephant in the living room no one wanted to acknowledge. Or they could address this while it was
still in its infancy, clear the air and move on.

She'd always been one to grab the bull by the
horns instead of leap over the fence, out of harm's
way.

C.J. set her mug down with a small thud, catching
his attention. "We've got to talk about it."

Warrick raised one eyebrow. "The case?" He
broke off a piece of the doughnut and popped it into
his mouth. A small shower of white powder rained
down to the floor. "That's why we're here."

He was playing games. "You know what I mean.
What happened last night."

Warrick looked at her pointedly. "Nothing happened last night. I was feeling a little protective, like
a big brother I guess, and you turned your head at
the wrong moment. We established that fact, remember?" He shrugged, washing the doughnut
down with a sip of coffee. "If you'd turned it the
other way, I would have gotten a mouthful of hair
instead of a mouthful of lip."

She scowled. "If I turned it the 'other' way, it
would have probably been part of an exorcism because that would have meant my head was turned
at a 180-degree angle."

He knew better than that, she thought, exasperated. Why was he pretending that they hadn't really
kissed, not like partners, certainly not like a brother
and sister, but like a man and a woman who wanted
each other? They both knew they had.

He gave a short laugh and put a little distance

between them, just for good measure. "There you go again, being contradictory. Arguing." His eyes held hers, his voice lowering, underscoring his words, his feelings. He wanted this buried. "Well, I don't feel like arguing, okay? Let's just do what we're being paid to do."

Warrick gestured at the main bulletin board, the one that displayed photographs of the victims, both before death had found them and after. Below each young woman was a list of statistics: name, age, height, weight, what the victim did for a living and where the body was found. So far none of that or any of the other endless pages of data they'd collected was giving them any clues that went anywhere.

The next moment, before she could answer him, they were no longer alone. Whatever was to have been said had to be set aside for now.

Culpepper poked his head into the room. "Was that the sound of raised voices I heard?" He walked into the room. "Back one day and you two are at it already, C.J.?" And then he looked at the conference table. His eyes lit up. "Ah, doughnuts."

He reached for one, but C.J. pulled the box away from him. He looked at her accusingly.

"Uh-uh, if you're going to insult me, you can't have any. I brought them."

Culpepper folded his hands together, palms touching and held them up before her. "A thousand pardons, oh wisest of the wise. That was just my sugar-deprived brain, running off with my mouth. If you were arguing, it was only because Warrick was provoking you.''

C.J. laughed and pushed the box toward the heavyset man again. ''Better.''

''No one was doing anything to anyone,'' Warrick told the other agent firmly. He slanted a look at C.J. to get his point across. ''Now feed your habit, Culpepper, and let's get to work on this.''

C.J. tossed her hair over her shoulder, ready to do battle. ''Fine with me. Let's nail this son of a bitch once and for all before he finds another victim.''

C.J. glanced at Warrick's profile, then lowered her eyes to her keyboard as he turned in her direction. Her fingers flew over the keys, drawing up screens she had already looked at a hundred times if not more.

She didn't know which was driving her crazier: the fact that after a few days the murder investigation seemed to have ground to a halt again—this despite phone calls coming in all hours of the day and night from helpful and not-so-helpful citizens who gave information that only led to dead ends, if they led anywhere at all—or that there was this restless tension intermittently buzzing through her. A restless tension that seemed to rear its head every time she and Warrick were near one another.

C.J. flipped to another screen, scrolling down. She knew this was stupid. Warrick was right, she argued with herself, absolutely right. Nothing had happened. After all, it wasn't as if he had actually *tried* to kiss her. It was a brotherly peck gone awry, that's all.

She hit the keys harder. She saw Warrick giving her a curious look. Damn it all, no brother she knew had ever kissed his sister like that.

Quietly C.J. took a deep breath. She had to get a grip on herself and let this die a natural death. After all, what was the big deal? Okay, so they had reacted to each other like a man and a woman. She hadn't been kissed by a man in almost nine months and he reacted like—well, like a man. All men took advantage of a situation if given the opportunity, some just less than others.

The kiss and her reaction had been an aberration, a freak of nature, like a thunderstorm in the wrong season, that's all.

Why was she letting it creep into each night and snare a toehold on each day?

C.J. looked over to the main bulletin board. Her eyes swept over the faces of the women there, women whose likeness were imprinted on her heart. Rising, she crossed to it.

She had no business even thinking about something so petty as a kiss at a time like this. Warrick was her partner, her backup, her friend, and she was his. That's all.

And that was enough.

Warrick looked at her over his computer. Her hands were clasped behind her back and she was studying the board intently.

"You're being quiet again," he observed. "It's

not like you. You make me nervous when you're quiet."

"Why, because you're afraid I'll pounce?" Not waiting for an answer, she turned from the board. "Just trying to get into the killer's head."

She looked over her shoulder, back at the board. Missing were the photographs of gruesome deaths, of savage beatings or stabbings. That wasn't the Sleeping Beauty Killer's style. Each victim was tenderly, perhaps even lovingly arranged. The latest victims even wore makeup that appeared to have been applied postmortem. They looked just like princesses waiting for their princes to come and wake them up. She chewed on her lips and looked at Warrick.

"You think he's a mousy man? You know, someone who yearns after the unattainable?"

He had never been able to crawl into a murderer's mind, maybe because he couldn't begin to identify with the kind of person who would willingly, sometimes even joyously take another human being's life. He marveled that C.J. could do it.

"Profiling's your department, not mine." Warrick moved over to the bulletin board with the map of Orange County on it. Each small pin designated a site where the victim was found. He wondered if there were going to be more pins before they caught the killer. "I just think he's one sick bastard." He looked at the blown-up photograph of the latest victim's nails. "Someone who obviously has a nail polish fetish."

Standing next to him, she studied the photograph

herself. "Maybe not a fetish. Maybe he's just trying to do something nice for them."

He caught a whiff of her perfume. Light, stirring. He wished she wouldn't wear it. Abruptly he directed his thoughts back to the conversation. "Not strangling them would have been nice."

Half aware of what she was doing, C.J. waved her hand at him, asking for silence. She was piecing this together as she went. "I mean like the kind of thing a guy would do for his girlfriend."

Culpepper came over to join them. "No guy I know paints women's fingernails."

C.J. frowned at the other man. "That's because every guy you know has just learned how to walk upright without scraping their knuckles on the ground."

"Hey," Rodriguez protested, walking into the room in time to catch the tail end of C.J.'s comment, "I take exception to that."

C.J. inclined her head toward the youngest member of their team. "Present company excepted, of course." She became serious again. "But what I'm talking about is when a guy tries to pamper a woman."

She looked from one man's face to the other and knew that as far as they were concerned, she was speaking a foreign language. She turned her focus on Rodriguez. After all, he was the one who was getting married and should be informed about this kind of thing. Her guess was that he was generally ignorant of the little niceties that women craved.

"You know, draw her bath, wash her hair for her

in the sink, do her nails." Nothing. Rodriguez's face was still blank, and Culpepper was laughing. She threw up her hands. "What am I, speaking in tongues here? Haven't any of you guys ever heard of pampering a woman?"

Culpepper stopped laughing. "That kind of thing really turns women on?"

She patted his chest. "Try it tonight on Adele and see."

He snorted, waving away the suggestion. "If I try washing her hair, she'll probably think I was trying to drown her."

"You're not supposed to drag her by her hair to the sink," C.J. pointed out, then shook her head as she looked at Warrick. "See what I mean? Neanderthal. I rest my case."

Warrick had the impression she was saying more to him than the actual words conveyed. But then he told himself to knock it off, he was starting to babble in his head.

Wanting to kiss a woman did that to a man.

He shut his mind down.

Culpepper regarded her with blatant curiosity in his eyes. C.J. thought for a second that perhaps she had a convert. "How about you, Jones? Does that kind of thing turn you on?"

She might have known better. This was getting a bit too personal. "Solving murders turns me on."

"Oh, tough lady," Culpepper deadpanned.

"Yes, and don't you forget it," she cracked, returning to her desk. She wondered if another canvass of the area where the last victim was found would yield anything. Maybe someone remembered something they hadn't mentioned the first time around.

She felt as if they were going in circles.

"Hey, Jones," Rodriguez called. "I almost forgot. It's your turn to field the crank calls."

She groaned, rising again. The more time that passed since the murder, the higher the ratio of crank calls to actual informative ones. "What are they down to? A hundred a day?"

Rodriguez sat down at his own desk. "Give or take."

She groaned louder as she walked into the adjacent room.

Chapter 7

"How about Hannah? Are you a Hannah?"

C.J. looked down at her daughter, trying out yet another name on her. The christening had been postponed because Father Gannon had suddenly been called away on personal business. His aged mother in Ireland was ill and not expected to recover. She could, of course, go with another priest, but she had her heart set on Father Gannon. She could wait. And while she waited, she continued searching for that elusive middle name.

Wide blue eyes looked back at her. Picking the baby up, C.J. patted the small, dry bottom.

"No, huh? How about Annie? Annie do anything for you?" She held the baby away from her, peering at the almost perfect face, trying to envision her daughter responding to the name. "Nothing." C.J.

tucked her against her left hip. "Okay, Desiree, how about that one? No, you're right, it's all wrong. Napoleon's mistress after Josephine, what are we trying to say here, right?" She sighed. "Let's forget about this name game for now and get you some breakfast, Joy."

C.J. hummed softly to herself as she walked back into the kitchen, the baby nestled against her hip. Outside, the world was dressed in dreary shades of gray, a rainstorm threatening to become a reality at any moment. But it was Saturday and she wasn't going into work today. She intended to make the most of it and spend the day bonding with her daughter.

It amazed her how quickly this little person had become such an integral part of her life. She couldn't begin to imagine life without her now.

The baby seemed to be growing a little each day right in front of her eyes. Each stage filled C.J. with wonder, but made her feel nostalgic, as well, something she would never have thought she'd experience. Nostalgic for the precious, small person she'd held against her breast, even though it had only been two short months since she was born.

Looking at her daughter, C.J. laughed softly to herself. "I don't know, Baby, I've turned into a real marshmallow when it comes to you." She opened the refrigerator and took out a bottle of milk, then placed it on the counter. Maybe she'd just name her Babe and be done with it. Naw. "If I feel this way now, what am I going to do when you want to start dating? Hanging out to the wee hours of the morning with who knows what kind of characters. And all they'll want is—''

C.J. stopped abruptly. Something akin to a revelation came to her. What she was feeling had been felt by mothers since the beginning of time. What her own mother must have gone through with her. She'd been more than a handful, determined to stay out as late as her brothers had, eschewing curfews.

Wow. Her poor mother. ''Omigod, honey, I think I owe your grandmother a great big apology.''

With the baby still tucked against her hip, C.J. picked up the telephone and dialed her parents' phone number with the same hand. She'd discovered she had an aptitude for doing a great many things with just one hand if she needed to, the other being recruited for far more precious work. Necessity was truly the mother of invention.

She heard her mother's voice on the other end of the line. ''Hello?''

''I'm sorry.''

There was a slight pause on the other end. ''Chris, is that you?'' Concern filled her mother's voice. ''Honey, what's wrong?''

''Yes, it's me.'' She hadn't meant to scare her mother. ''Nothing's wrong, Mom. I just wanted to call you to say I'm sorry.''

A note of confusion entered Diane's voice, even as the concern lingered.

''Why, what did you do? Chris, are you sure you're all right?'' Her voice began to escalate as countless scenarios occurred to her. ''You're not in any hostage situation are you? God, I wanted you to go into your father's firm instead of this cloak-and-dagger business. Why wouldn't you listen to me for just once in your life? You were always too independent—''

C.J. found her opening as her mother took a breath. ''Mom, slow down. I'm not in any hostage situation. I'm standing right here in my kitchen with the baby on my hip and—''

''She's not a rag doll, C.J.'' her mother admonished. ''Use both hands.''

C.J. rolled her eyes. ''Mom, can I just get this out, please?'' She said the words in a rush before the next interruption could occur. ''I'm sorry for everything I put you through while I was growing up.''

''You're forgiven.'' Her mother's concern took another direction. ''You're not ill or anything, are you, Chris? Should I come over?'' Not waiting for a response, she obviously made up her mind. ''Give me a minute, I'll just turn off your father's breakfast and—''

''Mom,'' C.J. raised her voice. ''Mom, stop letting your imagination run away with you. I'm fine, the baby's fine, I just suddenly had momlike feelings, and I realized what you must have gone through all these years with all of us. With me,'' she added after a beat. ''And I just wanted to tell you that I'm sorry for the grief I gave you.''

''Well.'' She heard her mother sighing a sigh she'd obviously kept in for years. ''I'm glad I lived to see the day.'' There was no pause whatsoever as she asked, "Now, does she have a middle name yet?"

Time to retreat, C.J. thought. "I've got to go, Mom, there's a call coming in on the other line. Talk to you later, bye."

She heard her mother sigh, murmur goodbye and then hang up.

"Okay, young lady, we were about to get you some breakfast before I had that unprecedented qualm of conscience." She cocked her head, looking at her daughter again. "Are you a Joy Michelle? No, that's not right, either."

With a sigh she opened the microwave door and reached for the bottle. The phone rang. Now what?

"This'll just take a minute," she promised her daughter. Picking up the receiver, she wedged it against her head and shoulder as she returned to the microwave. "Hello?"

Warrick was on the other end. His voice was grim. "There's been another murder, C.J."

She didn't have to ask if this concerned their killer. Her stomach instantly tightened.

Letting out a breath, she punched in one minute, three seconds and pushed the start button. "Where?"

"In Santa Barbara."

She frowned. That didn't sound right. "Santa Barbara? Is our boy spreading out?" God, she hoped not. C.J. shivered.

"That's what I'm going up there to find out."

Where was this coming from? "Not without me you're not."

''This is just a courtesy call, C.J. I figured you'd want to know. Stay home and take care of your baby.''

C.J. frowned. This was getting old. Ever since she'd returned to work, Warrick had been treating her differently. Not as an equal, but like someone who needed protecting. She didn't know if it was because of the kiss that shimmered between them like a silent entity, or because of the baby, but either way, she didn't like it and she wasn't about to stand for it.

''Warrick, this is my case just as much as it is yours. Now just give me a few minutes to get some things together so I can take the baby over to my mother's. I can be there in—'' she realized she didn't have enough information to make a time estimate ''—where are you?''

''I'm still at the field office. But C.J., there's no need—''

The microwave bell went off. She opened the door, then drew out the arm that was supporting her baby just far enough to test the temperature of the milk on her wrist. Perfect. Unlike this conversation.

''Yes, there is a need,'' she insisted. ''I have a need.'' Moving the chair away from the table with her foot, she sat down, then shifted the baby onto her lap. Cradling her daughter to her, she began feeding the infant, all the while never losing an ounce of her indignation. ''Damn it, Warrick, I'm still the same partner you always had.''

''No, you're not.'' His voice was low, steely. Unmovable. ''You're someone's mother now.''

That didn't warrant the preferential treatment. "And as someone's mother, I want to catch this bastard before he robs some other mother of her child." She smiled at her daughter, keeping her own voice calm so as not to frighten the baby. But it wasn't easy when her temper was flaring this way. "Now stop treating me as if I was made of porcelain and give me the courtesy of waiting for me to get there."

Soft tone or not, he knew C.J. well enough to know she was mad as the proverbial wet hen. "I'm not sure I want to do that now. You sound like you're breathing fire."

"You bet I'm breathing fire," she said between clenched teeth, her smile never wavering. "I worked long and hard to get here and I'm not about to give it up because you suddenly feel the need to treat me with kid gloves. I wouldn't treat you any differently if you had a baby."

She heard him laugh. Even though she was angry, the sound rippled against her ear, undulating through her. Did postpartum syndrome include hallucinations?

"If I had a baby, the *world* would treat me differently."

The baby was chugging away at the bottle, draining it like a trouper. At this rate, C.J. estimated, she would double her size in no time.

"Very funny. Now let me get off the phone and do what I have to do. And you'd better be waiting for me when I get there or I swear I will fillet your skin off your body when I get my hands on you."

She heard him laugh again. "Love it when you

talk dirty like that. Okay, I'll wait. Just don't take too long.''

C.J. hung up. The bottle was empty. She put the baby over her shoulder and just before she began burping her, she hit the speed dial to call her mother and switched to speakerphone. Multitasking had become a way of life for her.

She heard the phone being picked up. "Mom? Guess what—''

Thirty-five minutes later, C.J. was dashing off the federal building elevator and into the task force room.

Warrick was the only one in there. He looked up as she entered. "You look winded.''

She was winded. There had been no need to pack up anything, her mother had spares of all the necessary items for the baby. She'd made the trip from her house to her mother's in record time. For once, every light was with her. The hardest part was leaving the baby. You'd think it would get easier with each day, she thought, but it didn't. Some days it just got harder.

Still, C.J. waved away his observation. She was eager for news. "Never mind my wind, what have we got?''

He handed her a picture that had come in over the fax less than an hour ago. "Sally Albrecht, twenty-three, blond, blue-eyed, strangled, poetically arranged, pink nail polish.''

She nodded grimly, taking the photograph from him. This wasn't the kind of thing any of them welcomed hearing. She studied it for a moment. Like all the others, the latest victim appeared as if she were sleeping.

"Sounds like our boy's gotten tired of the local area and is making his way up the coast." Putting the fax down on her desk, she crossed to the map that had a tight little circle of pins on it. She'd been hoping that they could keep narrowing the circle, not widen it. Usually, serial killer victims were all over the map. This was supposed to make it easier for them. It didn't.

When she turned back from the map, she was frowning. "I don't like it. This blows the whole theory to pieces that he's a local guy."

"I know." He'd signed out a Bureau vehicle in the last half hour. Ready to go, Warrick gave her one last chance to change her mind. "You sure you don't want to stay home?"

He was just trying to be kind, she told herself. She had to remember that and stop taking offense where none was intended. There was no doubt in her mind that if he had some personal reason impeding him, she'd be trying to get him to stay behind.

C.J. nodded. "I'm sure. After my mother finished complaining that the Bureau doesn't let me have a life, she was thrilled to have to watch the baby."

"I've got a company car waiting downstairs. Let's go."

Walking through the office door first, Warrick didn't bother holding it open. C.J. put her hand out in time to keep it from shutting on her. "Hey!"

Warrick looked at her innocently. "You said not to treat you any differently from any of the other guys, remember?"

She strode past him to the elevator and punched the down button. "I don't recall you slamming the door in any of their faces."

"No slamming," he pointed out. "Just every man for himself."

"Person," she corrected as the elevator arrived and opened its doors. C.J. walked in ahead of him. "Every person for themselves."

Warrick followed her in and sighed. He pressed for the first floor. "I got a feeling this is going to be a long road trip."

Santa Barbara was approximately 150 miles north of the county that had previously been the Sleeping Beauty Killer's stomping grounds. Ordinarily C.J. loved driving up the coast, but the unexpected rain with its gloom made the trip dreary.

They'd flipped a coin, and Warrick had lost the toss. Taking the keys, he'd gotten behind the wheel of the midsize vehicle the Bureau had provided.

C.J. settled back in her seat and stared straight ahead. The rain was almost mesmerizingly hypnotic, causing everything farther than twenty feet away to appear surreal.

"You know, it's funny, but I miss her." She glanced at Warrick to see if he was laughing. He wasn't. "When I'm on the job, I find myself missing her, and when I'm home, my mind keeps going back to the case."

That was the complaint of more than one special agent. He could feel the car beginning to climb. Warrick swallowed to relieve the pressure in his ears. "Welcome to the world of parenthood."

She laughed shortly, shifting in her seat. Rain made her restless. Or maybe it was this case. "How would you know?"

He shrugged. "I read a lot." Moving with the curve in the road, Warrick spared her a glance. "You know, Rodriguez could just as easily have come with me."

C.J. thought the man was a good agent, but he liked his weekends to himself. "Rodriguez is still in love. Leave him with his fiancée."

Driving was getting a little trickier. Warrick slowed their speed down to a careful thirty-five miles an hour. "Well, Culpepper isn't in love." Not the way the man liked to complain about his wife, although Warrick suspected that there was a measure of affection in the grousing. "I know he would have been more than happy to make the trip to Santa Barbara."

C.J. looked at him incredulously. "You telling me that you'd rather have Culpepper sitting here next to you than me?"

For an optimistic woman, she had a habit of twisting his words to give them a darker meaning. "No, I'm telling you that it would have been okay for you to sit this one out."

C.J. wished he'd stop trying to make things easy on her. How could she feel like his equal if he kept insisting on spreading out his cloak for her so she could walk over the puddles without getting her shoes dirty?

"No," she told him quietly, firmly, "it wouldn't have."

"C.J. you're a new mother—"

Not that again. "Not so new," she contradicted. "Sure, I'm a mother now, but I'm also a special agent with the FBI." And that was very important to her. She'd had to buck not just her mother, but her father as well to get to where she was. And that didn't begin to take in the male agents along the way who resented having a woman on equal footing with them. In many ways it was still a man's world. "It's who I am and I'm damn proud of it. I've just got to find the proper balance to this combination, that's all. And you throwing up roadblocks all the time isn't exactly helping."

What was the use? thought Warrick. Mules had nothing on C.J. He slowed down more as a car, traveling in the opposite direction, its tires plowing through large puddles, sent an even heavier shower of water their way. For a second the windshield was obscured. Rain brought out the nutcases, he thought, all driving as if they had something to prove.

"I'm not throwing up roadblocks," he told her. "And I thought I was helping."

"Think again."

They needed a break. His eyes on the road, Warrick switched on the radio. He wanted some music to take the place of their voices.

She frowned at his selection and changed the station.

He switched it back, then batted away her hand when she reached for the dial again. "I'm driving, I get to pick the music."

"I'm driving on the way back."

He didn't bother looking her way. "Deal."

Crossing her arms in front of her, C.J. settled back in her seat again and watched the rain fight an endless skirmish with the windshield wipers.

She could never get used to it, C.J. thought. The smell of the bleak, dismal area where the Medical Examiner did his gruesome work permeated her senses even as she tried to breathe through her mouth.

The victim's body had been taken to the morgue. The local coroner had held off on the mandatory autopsy until the FBI special agents could get there. The moment they'd gone to the sheriff's office, the man had brought them here.

C.J. tried to divorce herself from the fact that the body on the table had been a person with aspirations and dreams under a day ago. Someone's daughter, someone's sister. She succeeded only marginally. Glancing at Warrick's profile, she saw that it remained stoic. Didn't he have any feelings?

Steeling herself, she approached the table.

"When was the time of death?" Warrick asked the heavyset man in the white lab coat.

The M.E., a Dr. Hal Edwards, glanced at the notes on his clipboard before answering.

"As near as I can place it, about fifteen hours ago." He flipped the pages back in place, retiring the clipboard to a desk. "I hate to tell you this," he looked from one to the other, "but you've probably figured it out already. Most of the clues have been washed away. It's been raining steadily here for the past few hours."

"Who found the body?" C.J. asked. She resisted the desire to brush back the victim's hair. There were no signs that the woman had suffered. She supposed that was some consolation to the victim's family, although not much.

"A jogger running for cover stumbled over her in the park. Called the police."

"Man?" Warrick wanted to know. It was not unheard of to have a killer take a life then pretend to be the first one on the scene to try to avoid suspicion.

"Woman. They had to give her a sedative to calm her down."

C.J. couldn't take her eyes off the girl's face. "God, she looks like a kid."

"We've got a positive I.D." the M.E. told her. "She was older than she looked." This time he didn't refer to his notes. The facts were still fresh. "Waitress in a local restaurant. No priors, decent girl. Engaged to be married. She looked like she fit the description of the Sleeping Beauty Killer's victims, so we called you." He recited the similarities. "Bruising around the neck, died of asphyxiation, pink nail polish."

C.J. carefully circled the girl, moving away from the M.E. The marks around the girl's neck were dark, ugly. She could almost feel the killer's hands around her own throat, literally choking the life out of her. C.J. shivered, looking down at the girl's hand. Something nagged at her. She picked it up to examine it.

The polish looked darker than the others had been. She looked closer.

Putting the lifeless hand down again, C.J. raised her eyes to the other two occupants in the room. Both men were looking at her. "This isn't his work."

The M.E took exception. He gestured toward the body. "The MO matches."

Warrick always teased her about her hunches, but 75 percent of the time C.J. was right. He'd learned to take her seriously. "You think someone else killed her?" C.J. nodded.

"She was found the same way," the M.E. pointed out. "On her back, hands folded around a rose. Choker around her neck."

That was it, she realized, what had bothered her when she looked at the fax the police had sent. "What kind of choker was it again?"

Edwards referred to his clipboard, scanning through two pages before answering. "Cameo."

Warrick shook his head. "Our boy uses cheap costume jewelry. Pearls." He glanced at C.J. "What made you realize this wasn't our serial killer?"

She held up the victim's hand. "I think the nail polish is just a coincidence. It's the wrong shade. More important than that, it's chipped. Our killer puts it on after they're dead." Her expression was grim. "Not much chance of chipping then."

Placing the hand respectfully beside the body, she moved around to the victim's feet. C.J. raised the sheet. "And also, it matches her toes. None of the others had painted toenails." She draped the sheet back over the victim's feet and looked up at the coroner. "I'm afraid it looks like you've got yourself an independent copycat murder, Dr. Edwards."

Chapter 8

The rain was coming down harder, beating down on all sides of the car.

C.J. looked at her partner as he carefully guided the vehicle. "Think whoever killed that girl is a groupie?"

They'd gone back to the sheriff's office after leaving the coroner and told the man their findings. Signing off on the case, they'd gotten back on the road within the hour, stopping only long enough to get something to go from a fast-food restaurant. The crumpled-up wrappers were now tucked inside the greasy paper bag on the floor behind her.

Warrick's hands tightened on the steering wheel. Despite their earlier agreement about C.J. driving back, she had deferred to him. Much as it pained her to admit it, of the two of them, he was the better driver.

It wasn't easy holding his own against the weather, Warrick thought. The roads were tough to negotiate and getting tougher by the minute. Rather than let up as the weatherman had predicted, the rain was coming down progressively harder.

"Maybe, maybe not." There were a lot of reasons to make the murders appear similar. "Maybe just someone looking to kill Sally and throw the blame somewhere else." He figured that was the most likely reason. The car kept swerving as the wind picked up. Keeping in his lane had become a monumental challenge. The lines were all but obliterated by the rain. "What I do think is that we'd better get ourselves an ark or get off this damn road. This stuff doesn't look like it's going to stop coming down."

C.J. frowned. Visibility was getting worse and worse as the windshield wipers, set on high, were clearly losing their battle with the rain. Except for precious single moments right after a pass, the rain had all but obscured the windshield.

To back up his suggestion, he added, "I remember passing a motel just on the outskirts of the city. After that, there's nothing for miles." He looked at her. It was their only alternative, but he left it up to her. "What do you want to do?"

"What I *want* to do is get home." C.J. pressed her lips together, frustrated. There was no way they were going to make it tonight. "But the sensible thing to do, I guess, is get a couple of rooms for the night and get an early start in the morning."

He nodded. He had slowed down considerably. The vehicle was barely crawling as it was. At this rate the trip would take more than twice the time.

"The rain might not let up by morning, but at least there'll be some light to help us see something." Warrick slanted a quick glance at her before gluing his eyes back on the windshield. Not that it helped all that much. "No sense tempting fate."

They'd already avoided one near accident just after the fast-food restaurant. A big rig, going the opposite way, had swerved, taking up too much of the road. They'd had to quickly scramble to the side, into what would have been a dirt shoulder. Because of the rain, it had almost become a river of oozing mud. Her heart was still trying to recover from the scare.

But weren't they tempting fate in a different way, stopping at a motel like this?

C.J. squelched her uneasiness. There was clearly no other sane choice. Besides, they were both adults, both sensible. In addition, they'd be in separate rooms. No reason to worry.

A smear of lights broke across the right corner of the windshield. C.J. squinted.

"There it is," she said, "that's the motel—I think." At this point it was difficult to identify anything positively.

"I see it."

Warrick slowed the vehicle even more, practically inching his way over as he searched for the entrance to the motel's parking lot. Finding it, he traveled approximately two feet before abruptly stopping the car.

"What's wrong?" C.J. asked.

"Is it me, or is that parking lot a lake?" From what he could make out, the center of the lot appeared to be underwater. "I think we'd better stop right here." Warrick pulled the vehicle over to the side as far as he could.

C.J. realized they had no choice but to get out and make a run for it to the rental office which, according to a neon sign, was directly beneath an arrow and off to one side.

She shook her head. "This is just getting better and better."

"We could spend the night in the car."

C.J. looked at him. The quarters were much too close for comfort of any kind, mental or physical. "You're kidding, right?"

"Right." Warrick put his hand on the door handle. "I'm beginning to appreciate the title *A River Runs through It.*" He looked at her. "Ready?"

She braced herself, then nodded and swung open her own door. The wind nearly pushed it closed again. Shoving, she made it out of the car. A gust of wind, pregnant with rain, hit her square in the face the moment she was out. Her ankles were instantly submerged in dirty water. The parking lot was rising.

Was the area prone to flash floods? She had no idea.

Her heart hammering, C.J. began to fight her way to the walkway that ran along the perimeter of the motel. The water tugged at her shoes. She tugged back with each step she took. Losing her footing, she slid and suddenly found herself meeting what would have been the ground if it hadn't been submerged.

The next second she was being pulled back up to her feet by her arm.

"Stay behind me," Warrick shouted to her over the howl of the wind. For once, he noted, she offered no resistance, no rebuttal. Using his body as a shield, he held her by the hand, keeping her well behind him as he made his way to the rental office and shelter.

Pulling the door opened, he pushed C.J. in ahead of him and shoved the door shut. They took a second to catch their breaths and get their bearings.

The dank smell of wet wood assaulted their noses. There was limited light in the office, coming from the yellowed fluorescent fixture overhead. Comprised of three long bulbs, the two closest to the door were out. There was an ancient TV set perched on a tall crate in the back. The blurry image of a sitcom was scattering itself all over the screen. The set had dials.

The small, thin clerk slowly uncurled himself from his position on the chair in front of the set and made his way over to the front desk. His eyes slid over C.J. slowly before he spoke.

"What can I do for you folks?" He was smirking as he asked the question.

"We'd like a couple of rooms," Warrick told him.

The man shook his bald head. "Sorry, no can do. All's I got is one left." He winked broadly at Warrick. "This *is* Saturday night, you know. Busiest night of the week."

"On a night like this?" The wind rattled the window to underscore C.J.'s point.

The man's smile was smarmy. "Hey, nothin' stands in the path of grabbing a little true love for an hour or two." Small, dark eyes moved from one to the other like little black marbles. "But then, I don't have to tell you two that, do I? I mean you're here, aren't you?"

"Not by choice," C.J. muttered.

Warrick sighed and took out his wallet. He put a fifty-dollar bill on the counter, keeping his fingertips solidly on the edge of it in case the man had any ideas about just grabbing the money.

"You sure there's only one room?"

The clerk's eyes were fastened to the bill. "I'm sure. If you want two, put another Franklin down on top of that one and I'll let you have my room for the night."

Warrick looked at C.J. "What do you want to do?"

There was nothing else *to* do. She was positive that the clerk's room probably had to be disinfected before it was inhabitable. She blew out a breath. "Give us the room."

The clerk cackled. "That's it, honey, you play hard to get. Men like a challenge, long as you don't make it too hard." He winked. "If you know what I mean."

Warrick saw C.J. clenching her fists at her sides. He felt like punching the clerk himself. The weather and circumstances had made him irritable.

"Just give us the key and spare us the philosophy," he ordered.

The clerk put his smudged fingers on the other end of the bill and waited. Warrick released it. Tucking it into the pocket of his baggy, mud-colored pants, the clerk turned and took the last remaining key off the pegboard to his left. He slapped it on the counter, then took a step back as if he was afraid of getting hit. "Yes, sir. Room 10. Dead center. Can't miss it."

She didn't appreciate the word *dead*. C.J. tugged on Warrick's arm. "Let's just go, Warrick. I'm dying to take a hot shower."

The clerk cleared his throat, still eyeing Warrick warily. "Oh, sorry, can't accommodate you there. The shower's not working. But the sink's got water," he added brightly, then a wicked smirk came over his lips. "You could always sponge each other off."

The glare Warrick gave the man had him backing farther away from his desk, his hands raised in mute surrender, his eyes fearful.

"Or not," he added in a mumble.

The shower wasn't working. Somehow that only seemed par for the course. C.J. turned away from the desk.

"Great," she muttered to Warrick. "It'll be like washing up in a birdbath." She didn't appreciate the fact that her partner looked as if he was struggling not to laugh.

Warrick opened the door for her. "Let's go."

He didn't have to say it twice.

They fought their way outside and down the cracked walkway. The red clay roof that jutted out overhead offered next to no shelter. The rain was lashing at them from all directions, swirling around almost like a whirlpool.

Water was lapping over the edges of the thin sidewalk, but most of the walkway wasn't submerged. Warrick looked over his shoulder to make sure that C.J. was still behind him. "Doing okay?"

His question, served by the wind, seemed to sweep over her like a physical entity. "Just peachy. Keep walking."

He couldn't hear her. The wind was stealing her words. He cupped his hand over his ear. "What?"

In reply, C.J. planted her hands against his back and pushed him forward. "Keep walking!"

"Good idea."

When they reached number 10's door, Warrick put the key the desk clerk had given them into the lock. Turning it took a bit of finesse. He jiggled it slightly and felt rather than heard a click.

"Maybe he gave us the wrong key," C.J. guessed, raising her voice. In which case she was going to go back and strangle the man.

"No, I think it's giving." Jiggling the key again did nothing. Warrick finally wound up pushing the door open with his shoulder. "Flimsy."

"Well, that makes me feel secure," C.J. commented, rushing into the room. She shook off as much of the rain as she could once she was inside.

Flipping on the light switch next to the entrance, Warrick shut the door behind them and looked around the room. "All the comforts of home."

"Yeah, if home's a brothel." Scarlet seemed to be the color of choice for the decor. There were dusty, sagging scarlet drapes, a scarlet bedspread that was worn in several places and scarlet lamp shades perched on small, erotic-looking lamps. "Who the hell did the decorating for this place, Hookers R Us?"

Warrick laughed. The room did go a long way in negating any kind of a romantic mood that might have been created by the rain. He only wished he could maintain that frame of mind. Soaking wet, C.J. still looked better than she should.

He stripped off his jacket and his shirt and walked into the adjacent bathroom to hang them up on the curtain rod. With any luck, they'd be dry by morning.

"Look on the bright side," he told her. "At least it's dry and the power's still on."

The wind was rattling the windows, which looked none too secure in their casings. "For now," C.J. qualified.

She wished he'd kept his shirt on. Or that his chest was flat and pasty like so many other men's were. But he was a walking testament to the hours he spent in the gym working out. She walked by an oval mirror hung over a broken-down bureau. One of its handles was gone. The silver all along the bottom of the mirror had begun to peel away.

But she saw enough to make her cringe. "God, is that mud in my hair?"

Warrick came up behind her and began examining the top of her head. When she tried to bat away his hands, he batted back. "I'm only trying to help. No, no mud, it looks like twigs." He laughed. "Thinking of starting a nest?"

"Very funny." C.J. shook her head, brushing the twigs out with her fingers. She made a point of moving away from Warrick and his bare chest. She looked toward the bathroom. "My kingdom for a shower."

"There's always the sink. The clerk said it was working." Walking back into the bathroom, he turned the faucet on. After making one sputtering noise, water began to flow. "At least he didn't lie about that." Rain was lashing at the small bathroom window. "Or you could always stand outside with a bar of soap."

Now there was an idea, she thought cynically. "The clerk would probably charge admission." Moving past Warrick, careful not to brush against him, she turned on the shower taps. Nothing happened.

With a sigh she looked at the sink. Better than nothing. "At least I could wash my hair—if I had some shampoo." This was not going down as one of her better days. "I didn't exactly pack for an overnighter." When she turned from the shower, she saw Warrick squatting down in front of the sink, rummaging through the faded yellow cabinet. "What are you doing?"

"Finding you some shampoo." He held his trophy up for her to see. It was a half-empty bottle of pink liquid.

She looked closer. "That's dishwashing liquid."

Rising, Warrick looked at the bottle, then shrugged. "Soap's soap." He arched an amused brow. "Beggars can't be choosers."

She took the bottle from him, resigned. "I hate it when you're right."

His mouth curved. "You must spend a lot of time being upset."

"In your dreams."

The deep-scarlet towel on the rack beside the sink was surprisingly fluffy. She placed it within easy reach. C.J. turned in the collar of her shirt so it wouldn't get in the way and then turned on the water. Testing it with her fingers, she waited until the water temperature was fairly decent, then lowered her head. She angled it under the faucet to wet her hair with clean water.

"Might have gone faster for you if you stuck your head out the door," Warrick observed. Her only answer was to sigh. Crossing his arms before his chest, he leaned against the doorjamb and watched her begin to lather her hair.

The tawdry surroundings began to fade into the background. There was something almost sensual about what she was doing, her fingers working up a lather, working it through her hair.

He could feel that same stirring again within him. The nameless one he didn't want to dwell on.

"This whole trip's been a bust," she told him, raising her voice in case he couldn't hear her above the running water. "I hope there's a signal in here. I've got to call home. Otherwise, my mother's going to have the state troopers looking for both of us. Kind of funny, really. Here we are, two special agents with the FBI, trained to the hilt in self-defense and there's my mother, probably worrying about us getting lost in the rain."

Suddenly she felt another set of hands beginning to massage her scalp. She started. "What the—"

Gently, Warrick pressed her back down. She was as skittish as a cat, he thought. He could see the tension all through her shoulders. Not that he was supposed to be noticing that about her.

"Relax," he soothed. "It's just me."

Just him, right. Just as it was "just raining" outside. A more apt description was monsooning. And there was no "just" about Warrick.

Drawing on anger, she worked to steady her pulse. "What the hell do you think you're doing?"

"Testing your theory," he answered. Definitely sensual, he thought as he continued massaging her hair. "I thought you said women liked having a man do this sort of thing."

"They do. We do," she corrected before he could make a comment about her excluding herself from the gender. "But what do you know about washing hair?"

"I wash my own. How much different can this

be?'' He smiled at her back. ''Okay, now relax and
let me do this. You've been through a lot lately. I
thought I'd do something nice for you.''

She didn't want him doing something nice for her.
She was having a hard enough time thinking of him
as her partner and nothing more. Especially since
he'd taken off his shirt.

C.J. tried to twist away, but he held her body fast
against the sink. ''But—''

He laughed. ''Just shut up, Jones, and enjoy it,
okay? I am.''

She froze. It had to be the acoustics here in the
sink. She could have sworn he said he was enjoying
this, too. ''What did you say?''

That had just slipped out. His mind scrambled for
a plausible explanation. ''There's something thera-
peutic about immersing your hands in hot water and
suds.''

He's your partner, your partner. She chanted the
line in her mind like a mantra. ''Remind me to have
you around when I wash dishes.''

''You still wash dishes?'' He couldn't picture her
doing anything domestic. Trouble was, he was pic-
turing her a whole different way, which had nothing
to do with dishes and everything to do with suds.
He ran a tongue along dry lips. ''What about the
dishwasher?''

C.J. clung to the mundane topic. ''Wasteful.
There's never enough dishes to put in.''

He'd never noticed how inviting the slope of her
neck was, gently curving just enough for a man's

hand to hold while he was kissing her. "Maybe you should entertain more."

His voice was low, sultry and wreaking havoc on her nervous system.

"Maybe."

Why did it feel as if every word was sticking to the roof of her mouth? And why was she so aware of the heat coming from his body? The rest of the room wasn't warm. Or hadn't been when she'd entered.

He finally stopped just as she felt herself melting. The warm water caressed her scalp, washing away the lather. She dug her nails into her palms. It didn't help divert her attention.

She swallowed, trying her hardest not give herself away. "You're very good at this."

He worked a stubborn tangle out of her hair, then moved his fingers through the strands, making sure the soap was all out of it. "Thanks."

"You've done this before." Nobody was this good without practice. Had he done this for his ex-wife? A lover, maybe?

Jealousy flickered through her. Appalled, she shut it away.

"No. Just a natural, I guess. There." He shook off his hands. "Done."

She raised her head, looking at him oddly as she wrung out the remaining water from her hair with her hands. Taking the towel, she blotted her face and neck before lowering her head again in order to wrap the towel around it like a turban.

She raised her head. The light in the room wasn't

bright. It didn't matter. She could see the look in his eyes. It called to something within her.

Every pulse point within her body began to hammer.

Chapter 9

C.J. remained very still, not daring to take a breath, to blink an eye. Everything within her felt as if it had suddenly frozen.

"Warrick?"

"Yes?" He stood less than two feet away from her, his eyes never leaving her face.

His eyes were holding her captive. "What are you thinking?"

His voice was soft, low, each word carefully measured out, as if spilling it too soon was unthinkable.

"That this rain is never going to stop. That we should have gotten more take-out food when we had a chance." He moved forward. The two feet between them began to disappear until it was almost all gone. "And that I want to kiss you. Very much."

"Why don't you?" she whispered.

Very slowly Warrick ran his hand along her cheek, then cupped the back of her head and brought her lips halfway to his.

He met her the rest of the way.

His lips were hard, firm.

Gentle.

And they drew the very life out of her, creating something wild and uncontainable in its place. Heat surged all around her. Through her. She might as well have been standing in a sauna.

Abandoning any pretense that this wasn't affecting her, C.J. rose up high on her toes, as far as she could reach, falling deep into the kiss. Not wanting to miss a single nuance.

The towel slipped from her head onto the floor, completely unnoticed. All she was aware of was this fire burning within her.

Fire and craving.

His arms were around her, pulling her closer to him. She could feel the heat radiating from his bare chest.

At least she wasn't the only one in overdrive, she thought. A lot of good that did her.

This was bad, Warrick thought, really bad. Kissing C.J. hadn't satisfied anything. It just opened up the floodgates. Made him want her all the more.

For a man who liked to maintain control of every waking moment of his life, he found himself a hopeless captive of what was happening right now.

What was more, he didn't care.

Didn't care that things were twisting around him, didn't care that what he felt was so out of character it might as well have been happening to someone else. All he cared about was kissing her.

Having her.

The realization came like a crashing blow to his brain. He wanted to make love with her. With C.J. His partner.

This was getting way out of hand.

Drawing a deep breath, Warrick managed to separate himself from her. It almost surprised him to discover that there was an end to him and a beginning to her. For a moment he'd felt they had formed one continuous whole. One endless circle.

He struggled to pull himself together, to cover up what he was feeling. She looked dazed. That made two of them, he thought.

He took another step back and noticed the towel. "Um," he pointed to the floor behind her, "I think your turban fell."

Numbly C.J. turned to look where he was pointing. She stared down at the damp towel as if she didn't recognize what it was.

"Oh, right. It did."

How long had the room been spinning around like this? Though it was secretly humiliating, she held on to his arms a second longer. Trying to regain the use of her mind as well as her legs. Both became available to her in small increments. She took what she could get.

C.J. drew another deep breath, realizing that there was no air in her lungs. "I'd…I'd better call my mother." She dropped her hands to her sides.

''She'll be worried. And I need to check on the baby.'' Her throat had never felt this dry.

All the moisture seemed to have gone to other parts of her body.

Warrick stepped aside. After retrieving the towel, he handed it to her. Rather than wrap her hair again, she just toweled it dry as she walked into the other room on wobbly legs.

The room felt terribly cramped suddenly. It was dominated by the bed, and the scarlet walls began to close in on her.

She wished it wasn't raining so she could go out for a walk. But if it hadn't been raining, she wouldn't be here. They wouldn't be here.

Her head hurt.

Her body ached.

Taking out her cell phone, C.J. found the ever-annoying message written across her screen. The phone couldn't find a network. It wasn't receiving a signal. She looked around for Warrick. He was still standing in the bathroom doorway. Watching her.

She tossed her cell phone on the bed. ''Give me your cell phone.''

Crossing to her as he took the small silver phone out of his back pocket, he held it out to her. ''Why don't you just use the motel phone?''

She took the phone from his hand. ''It's probably just programmed for phone sex.''

C.J. glanced down at the cell phone's LCD screen. Warrick had a different service provider, but the message was the same. The storm was playing havoc with all manner of signals.

Hers included.

With a sigh C.J. handed him back his cell. "You're not receiving signals, either."

"Oh," he tossed the phone on the nightstand, a smile slipping across his lips, "I wouldn't exactly say that." And he had absolutely no idea what to make of them, or where to go from here.

Ignoring his comment, C.J. sat on the edge of the bed facing the regular phone. Gingerly she picked up the receiver and held it to her ear. The motel phone still had a rotary dial. Maybe whoever ran this place thought it was sexier. Or nostalgic. Or maybe they'd just been too cheap to replace the phones. Whatever the reason, it was inconvenient to use.

Deliberately blocking out Warrick, she dialed her mother's number.

The phone was picked up on the first ring. "Where are you?"

She was right. Her mother was worried. "That's not how you answer the phone, Mom," she chided, struggling to keep her voice level, grateful that she had this minor distraction to cling to. "What if this was an obscene phone call?"

"I'd hand it to your father," Diane said matter-of-factly. "And don't talk to me about phone etiquette. You should have been home by now, or called earlier. Where are you?"

C.J. ran her hands along her forehead where the ache was forming. *In Limbo, Mom. Halfway between heaven and hell.* "We're still in the Santa Barbara area. The storm's really bad up here."

As if to punctuate her statement, the wind picked up and rattled the windows and the door. It felt as if the breeze went right through the room. Mercifully, the rain didn't.

"It's no picnic here, either," her mother told her. "It's been coming down all afternoon and evening. So are you at a hotel?"

"Motel," C.J. corrected.

"Not a sleazy one I hope."

C.J. looked around at the scarlet furnishings. "No, not sleazy." This place was way beyond sleazy. On a scale of one to ten, it had fallen off the charts.

She heard her mother sigh with relief. "Good, I won't have to worry about you driving back in this. Wait until the rain lets up," Diane advised. "And don't worry about the baby. She's being a little fussy, but your father's having a ball with her. He thinks Joy's middle name should be Cynthia. What do you think?"

The only Cynthia she knew had stolen her boyfriend in college. The name did not hold pleasant memories. "We'll pick names when I get back, Mom."

Her mother sighed again, this time like a long-suffering saint. "Like I believe that. All right, she's your daughter. Tell Byron I said hello."

C.J. ran her tongue along her lips. It didn't help. They were as dry as dust. "If I see him," she murmured. "'Night mother. Kiss the baby for me."

"Already have. Bye."

She held the receiver a moment more, even though her mother was no longer on the other end.

When she finally hung up, Warrick was standing in front of her.

Tiny nerve endings all along her body came to life. Every single one of them was desperately telegraphing "Mayday" to her.

"Everything all right?" he asked. She had a strange look on her face. Maybe there was something wrong with the baby.

Nodding in slow motion, C.J. rose to her feet. She pushed the telephone back on the nightstand. She couldn't think, couldn't piece two thoughts together. She'd had one of the sharpest minds in her class at the Academy, and it was now the consistency of warm mutton.

"My mother says to say hi." She took a deep breath and looked up at him. "Hi."

"Hi," he answered softly.

Warrick slipped his hands around her waist.

She cleared her throat nervously. "I don't suppose there's anything on TV." C.J. glanced over at the ancient console against the wall.

"Cable's out," he told her. "I checked."

"Oh." She couldn't draw her eyes away from his face, from his mouth. "So now what do we do?" Each word found its way out slowly.

Her hair was curling around her head. He kind of liked that. "I thought maybe we could explore that kiss again."

He hadn't moved. How was it that he was closer to her than he'd been just a heartbeat ago? Or was she the one who was moving? "Do you think that's wise?"

"No." The admission was honest, skimming along her skin like a seduction. He brushed a wet curl aside, his lips lingering a moment on the curve of her neck. Sending shivers down her spine. "I'm not feeling very wise tonight."

"Me, neither," she murmured as she encircled her arms around his neck.

His lips found hers.

It was like an explosion. The instant his mouth made contact with hers, she felt as if all the stops had suddenly been pulled out. As if her entire body had launched into fourth gear without ever bothering to go through the other three.

As the storm continued to release its fury outside, another raged within the small room. Within her. All the safeguards, all the warnings she had so strictly issued to herself had been completely incinerated.

None of it mattered.

His mouth made all her thoughts, all her former protests null and void. Vaporizing them as if they'd never existed. The way he kissed her, tenderly, possessively, made her want to give herself to him without qualms, without reservations.

She just wanted him to make love with her.

To her.

They tumbled backward onto the bed, their lips still sealed to each other's. The urgency inside of her scrambled wildly in her chest, not for higher ground but for fulfillment.

Warrick could feel his heart slamming against his ribs like a jackhammer gone out of control. His mind was a jumble of thoughts, of fragments, very few of which made any sense at all.

Thoughts gave way to a higher order. Sensations were traveling through him, memories of sweet things, erotic things, all brought on by the taste of her lips, the promise of her body.

He ran his hands over her, striving not to be rough, succeeding only marginally.

As he pressed his lips against the hollow of her throat and heard her breath quicken, he worked away at the buttons on her blouse. Reining himself in to keep from ripping them off.

Undone, the material parted. Very lightly he ran his fingers along her skin. It quivered beneath his touch. Something quickened in his belly, the sensation echoing in his loins.

Over and over again he caressed the soft contours of her body, finding, exploring. Claiming. Feasting. He couldn't get enough. More just bred a desire for more. There was no end.

Warrick freed her from her blouse, tossing it aside. He pushed her back down against the lurid scarlet comforter, his mouth exploring the contours of her face, his fingers tugging away the straps of her bra.

One movement of his fingers and the barrier was gone. He covered her breasts with his hand, first one, then the other. The hairs along his arm gliding along her skin, making her twist and strain against him.

Her breasts were soft, tempting. Desire surged through him, hardening him further.

His hand was replaced by his mouth. It encircled each peak, his tongue lightly flicked against the small, hardening flesh.

C.J. moaned, arching, wanting. Her breath grew shorter. She undid his belt buckle, then the zipper on his pants, tugging the immediate material aside. She cupped him. He kissed her harder, making the flame grow.

She wiggled into him, pressing her body against his as he tugged away her skirt, leaving her in her underwear. Her heart was beating so hard she was having trouble breathing.

His hands were everywhere, caressing her, taking her. Heating her. Making her damp.

She tugged urgently on his pants, wanting to tear away the final barrier. "Damn it, get rid of them," she cried in frustration when they wouldn't go down any farther.

Rolling away from her, Warrick laughed softly, teasingly, his eyes devouring her body. She was nude except for the lacy next-to-nothing she still had on.

She was magnificent, he thought. Somehow, he'd always known she would be.

He kicked off his pants. "Your wish is my command."

"Not hardly," she countered as his mouth came down again on hers.

She tangled her fingers in the underwear he'd left on. It was small, covering just enough. Conservatively black. Somehow she'd known he wouldn't wear boxers. It excited her.

Everything about him excited her.

She kicked the last of her own underwear away after he'd teased them slowly down her legs.

With a cry that was half victory, half surrender, she turned into him.

He kissed her lips, her chin, her throat, his hands massaging her body as he slowly worked his way downward, covering her belly, her navel, until he found the very core of her.

Her eyes flew open as the first shock wave hit, undulating all through her with a force that sucked away her ability to breathe.

She dug her fingers into his shoulders, trying to anchor herself to something before she was swept away. This was something new, something she'd never experienced before.

Her body continued to hum as he drew himself up along her, his skin rubbing over hers.

When he rolled his body onto hers, she summoned every last stitch of strength she had and moved quickly. Catching him off guard, she reversed their positions. He was looking up at her. There was surprise in his eyes. Good. She grinned at him.

''My turn,'' she announced and proceeded to emulate the path he had taken on her body.

She succeeded royally in heightening both his arousal as well as her own. With each pass of her lips, each nip of her teeth, each teasing flick of her tongue, she could feel her excitement rising up to a fever pitch. Could feel him wanting her.

She felt triumphant.

She felt eager.

And then his hands were on her shoulders. Gently he dragged her up along his body until his eyes were level with hers.

"No more turns," he told her, his voice low, deep. The promise in it penetrated her very being.

With a movement that was every bit as swift as her own had been, Warrick was suddenly over her, his body less than a breath away from hers. Tantalizing them both.

He laced his fingers with hers and entered.

Warrick felt her tightening around him instantly. He drove himself further into her. Her sharp intake of breath echoed in his mouth as he kissed her hard and with all the passion that had flowered within him.

The dance began, going ever faster with each second that passed. They were both master and prisoner of the other, all at the same time.

The dance brought them to a plane that was miles above anything either of them had ever imagined. Ever experienced.

With a cry C.J. arched against him, silently imploring him to bring the final climax before she died from wanting.

They moved faster and faster, each following the other, each inspiring the other.

The last crescendo came, sweeping them up and

over the plateau they had discovered together. He thought she cried out his name; he wasn't sure.

And when it was over, when the afterglow descended, embracing them with misty arms that held fast, he rolled off C.J. and then gathered her to him with his last ounce of energy.

He'd never felt so drained and so good before in his life.

Warrick had no idea what that meant, or what to make of it. Maybe he was feeling this way because it had been a while since he'd been with a woman.

He didn't know.

All he knew was that he liked being here with this one. For now.

His arm tightened around her as he waited for the world to stop spinning around.

Chapter 10

He was watching her.

She looked so pretty, the way her long, blond hair swayed along her back when she walked. He'd heard someone call her Jackie, but they were wrong.

She was Claire. Claire had come back to him.

She had the same hair, the same eyes. The same smile. She was Claire no matter what they called her.

His Claire.

And he had to make her his again. Just like the last time. His so that that she couldn't tell him to leave her alone, couldn't call him a frog.

No, not a frog, a toad. That was it, a toad. She'd called him a toad, but he knew she didn't mean it.

She was too pretty to be mean.

And she would smile at him when he gave her

her present, he knew she would. A secret smile only he could see.

He put his hand into his pocket. The little pearls felt smooth and shiny beneath his fingers. He couldn't wait to give it to her.

And when she wore it, she'd be his again.

Forever.

Just like the last time.

C.J. stirred. There was something heavy on her chest, something keeping her from drawing in a deep breath. Eyes still closed, she tried to push it away and realized that it was an arm. A man's arm.

She pried her eyes open. Warrick.

C.J. sat bolt upright. "Oh, God."

Warrick's eyes flew open, instantly alert, scanning the immediate vicinity to see what had caused the exclamation that was echoing even now in his head.

And then he saw C.J. sitting up next to him, completely devoid of makeup, her hair rumpled. C.J. looking like the best thing he'd ever seen. The sheet she held against her exposed more than it hid.

The fight-or-flight tension left his body. Another tension, far more pleasant, entered, taking its place. He felt something stirring within him. Hunger for food took a back seat to a different, even more basic kind of hunger.

Last night returned to him in vivid shades that made the room's decor pale in comparison.

"'Morning." Propping himself up on his elbows, he lightly swept his fingers along her cheek, brushing back the hair that had fallen into her eyes.

Her heart again on double time, C.J. jerked her head away. Every single disastrous story about doomed relationships in the workplace filed by her in a snaking conga line that jolted her system. At the end of the line was her own dismal experience with Tom Thorndyke.

He'd been an FBI special agent, too.

What the hell had she been thinking last night?

That was just it, she hadn't been thinking. Not for one second. What she'd been doing was feeling, always a bad move on her part.

"Yes," she acknowledge testily, "it is."

His rock-hard chest seemed to be mocking her. In an effort to save herself, she glanced toward the window. The sun was pushing its way through the clouds like a merchant, late opening up his store, pushing his way through the gathered throng.

"The rain stopped," she announced needlessly. "We can get going now."

Warrick glanced at the wristwatch he never removed. It was almost seven. Seven on a Sunday morning. Even God rested on Sunday. He was in no mood to hit the road just yet. Far more enjoyable scenarios presented themselves to him than a three-hour road trip.

Maybe it was because he felt that once they left this room, this site of their unexpected aberration, they would go back to being partners. Partners and nothing more.

He wanted more.

Just within the confines of this gaudy room, he

wanted more. He wanted to hold on to last night for just a little longer.

Was that too much to ask?

He slid light exploring fingers along C.J.'s bare back and saw her shiver in response. Saw her eyes flutter closed before springing open again.

"What's your hurry?" His question sounded incredibly seductive.

Even as she stiffened, tiny sensations had begun marching through her body, picketing for a return to last night. There was no denying that it had been leagues beyond wonderful. But that was last night. In the light of day, things had to be different. *Were* different.

"Stop touching me," she told him.

Slowly, seductively he withdrew his fingers. "Why?" He watched her face. "Because you don't like it?"

She wanted to lie. It was easier that way. Easier for her, maybe even for him. But she couldn't. Not even to save herself. Not to Warrick.

"Because I do like it."

The smile that curved his lips was nothing short of sensual and worked its way instantly beneath her skin, heating it.

"I'm beginning to understand why your parents called you Christmas." Warrick sat up, then pressed a single, soft kiss to her shoulder. Sending skyrockets launching through her. "Open the package and there's something entirely different under the wrappings." Lifting the hair away from her neck, he pressed another kiss there. C.J. felt herself losing ground. Rapidly. "You were quite a revelation last night."

It was getting hard for her to think again. What *was* this effect he had on her?

"I wasn't myself last night."

She felt his lips curving against her skin. He was smiling. She could feel warmth flowing to every part of her.

"Any chance of your secret identity making a reappearance this morning?" he asked.

He was dissolving her will faster than a gale traveling through soap suds. It was a struggle just to keep her eyes from shutting, her body from sinking back down. Her protest barely carried conviction. "Warrick, we're on a case—"

"We're on a bed," he countered, working his way to the other side of her neck. Causing miniquakes in her stomach. "And once we go out of this room, it's going to be business as usual. I want to stay here with you like this a little longer, maybe make a few more memories to sustain me." She felt his breath along her back. Everything inside of her tightened in anticipation. Suddenly she was looking up into his eyes as he cupped her cheek. It took everything she had not to curl into his palm. "Is that so bad?"

"No," she breathed. From some dark region, a little voice urged her to remember the fiasco that resulted when she had been with Thorndyke. She snapped to attention. "Yes. Look, we can't do this."

He knew that she was probably right, knew all the arguments against this. Knew only one argument for it. Because he wanted her. Again. "Newsflash, we already *did* do this."

"Okay." She told herself to get up out of bed. That's all she needed to do. After all, this was Warrick. She knew him. He wouldn't force her to do anything she didn't want to do. Wherein lay her problem. Because she *did* want to. "We can't do this again."

"Why?" Straightening, he looked at her. Maybe they needed to say this aloud. "We're both adults, both know the rules of the game."

Right now, with Warrick touching her like that, looking at her like that, she wasn't sure she even knew her own name.

C.J. cleared her throat. It was impossibly dry. Where was saliva when you needed it? "And those are?"

"No strings. No promises. Just two consenting adults..." He smiled warmly into her eyes, touching her again. "Consenting."

She wondered what the melting point for people was. The way she felt, she was very nearly there. "No strings?" she echoed. That sounded good. In theory.

He nodded slowly, his eyes never leaving hers. "No strings. We both know that strings only tangle you up, make you trip."

"Right." He was absolutely right. So why did she suddenly want to start a string collection? Why this desire to gather together the world's biggest ball of twine? No, no, Warrick was right. They were two sane adults—hungering for a few insane moments.

Her heart was hammering too hard, surrendering the battle without a decent shot being fired. The next minute he had pulled her down until she was flat on her back and under him.

"Right," he echoed just before he brought his mouth down on hers.

The fire ignited a beat before his lips even touched hers. Anticipation had primed her response to him.

Primed her.

God help her, but she wanted this with every fiber of her being, even though she knew she shouldn't. In the light of day, with reason returning, she really shouldn't.

But she did.

The sound of bells began to peal in her soul, in her brain. Bells. Ringing.

The urgent sound took a moment before it penetrated. It took her a moment longer before she could identify it. Not bells, a cell phone. One of their cell phones was ringing.

Warrick had heard it, too. He lifted his head, drawing back. Impatience creased his forehead. They knew it could be important. He rose away from her, sitting back on his knees. "Yours or mine?"

"I don't know." They both rang the same. Sitting up, still more than a little dazed, she looked where both cell phones lay on the nightstand where they'd been left last night. Obviously, the signal problem had cleared itself up. Talk about bad timing.

She picked up his first, then hers. Hers had the lit screen.

''Mine,'' she told him. Taking a deep breath, she hoped that she didn't sound breathless as she felt. ''This is Jones.''

''Chris, it's Mom.''

Responses programmed before the beginning of time made C.J. pull the sheet up around her more tightly, covering her breasts. ''Hi, Mom, what's up?''

''The baby's temperature.''

''What?'' Alert, concerned, C.J. sat up, swinging her legs over the side of the bed. Behind her, she felt Warrick tap her on the shoulder, silently asking to be enlightened. She waved him back, her attention riveted to the voice on the other end of the line. Something was wrong with her baby. ''How high is it?''

Her mother didn't answer immediately, as if debating whether or not to tell her. ''A hundred and two.''

''Omigod.''

The bed moved behind her. Warrick came around it to face her. ''What is it?''

Shaking, she covered the receiver. ''The baby has a 102-degree temperature.'' C.J. removed her hand, her attention back to her mother. How was this possible? She'd left the baby in perfect health just yesterday morning. ''But she was all right when I called you last night.''

''Baby's temperatures can suddenly go up and just as suddenly go down again. I didn't call to panic you, Chris. I knew you'd want to know. I've got a call in to her pediatrician.''

Dr. DuCane had come with excellent references and she hadn't been disappointed when she'd met the woman. But this was her baby they were talking about. C.J. struggled to get ahold of herself.

"Maybe you should go to the emergency room with her, have the doctor meet you there." C.J. ran her hand over her forehead and tried to think. Why couldn't she think? Why was everything such a jumble in her head? She'd always been able to think on her feet before, that was her greatest strength. Up until now. "I'll be there as fast as I can."

"There's nothing you can do, honey," her mother told her. "Everything's being taken care of. I don't want you breaking any speed limits. Ethan had a fever of 106 once, and he's still with us." She recited chapter and verse from a book that had guided her through all five of her children's childhoods. "'Babies temperatures fluctuate all over the place until they're seven.'"

She didn't care about other babies, she cared about hers. And she needed to be there with her.

"I'll be there as soon as possible," C.J. reiterated. "Call me after you talk to the doctor."

Slapping the cover down on the phone as she ended the conversation, she realized that her hands were shaking. This having a baby was so much harder than she thought. Labor was only the beginning.

"Here."

C.J. looked up and saw that Warrick had gathered her clothes together and had placed them on the bed next to her. He was stepping into his underwear.

Even in the midst of a crisis, she couldn't help thinking that he had to have one of the most magnificent bodies she had ever seen. The next moment she upbraided herself. What kind of a mother *was* she, having the hots for someone while her baby was burning up?

''We can be on the road in fifteen minutes,'' he told her. She nodded in response. Something on her face must have caught his attention because he stopped after he pulled up his pants and buttoned them. ''She's going to be all right, C.J.'' She didn't remember ever hearing him sound so comforting. ''Babies get sick all the time.''

She snapped out of her stupor and began hurrying into her clothes. ''That's what my mother said.''

''She ought to know.'' He pushed his arms through his sleeves and quickly buttoned his shirt. ''She raised five of you.''

C.J. nodded, knowing she should have felt comforted. Knowing that all she felt was scared.

After one quick ten-minute stop at a drive-through for something that vaguely passed as breakfast, plus four containers of black coffee, they were on the road for home.

The tension inside the vehicle was almost tangible. There was tension because they hadn't had the opportunity to either redefine or renew the boundaries that they had crossed over last night, nor would they. Not until the reason for the preponderance of tension was resolved.

When they'd left the motel, C.J. had gone to the driver's side. Warrick blocked her and claimed the wheel. "I don't think you're in any condition to drive right now, and I don't have a death wish." He'd expected an argument. Instead she'd merely nodded her head and gone to the passenger side.

That was when he knew the extent of her concern.

The silence was making him uneasy. Warrick turned on the radio, selecting a station he knew she liked over one for himself. They had extremely different taste in music. Hers was modern, his leaned toward the oldies. Anything after 1970 was far too modern for him.

He glanced at her profile. If she was any more rigid, she would have qualified as granite. He pressed down on the accelerator. The speedometer climbed over the legal limit.

"She's going to be all right," he finally said, breaking the silence for the second time. He wasn't even sure she'd heard him the first time around.

I have to believe that, C.J. thought desperately. Anything else was unthinkable. Two months into the relationship and she couldn't imagine her life without her daughter. But she was so little....

C.J. clenched her hands in her lap as she tore her mind away from going through that door. She refused to allow herself to think of anything bad happening.

She slanted a look in his direction. There was something comforting about his smile. "Thanks," she whispered.

He glanced at the rearview mirror to make sure there were no police cars in the vicinity. The road had opened up and there were no other cars in either direction. "For what?"

Her nails were sinking into her palms. She unclenched her hands. "For not saying 'I told you so.'"

Where the hell had that come from? "Why would I say that?"

Didn't he remember? "You were the one who told me to stay home. Twice."

Warrick carefully negotiated a curve, then resumed his former speed. "And what…if you were home, the fever wouldn't have happened?"

He made the basis of her guilt and self-reproach sound foolish. "No, but—"

He didn't give her a chance to come up with an argument. The whole thing was ridiculous.

"And don't tell me that if you were home, you would have handled it any better than your mother's handling it right now. You probably would have called her for advice." When she said nothing, Warrick spared her a look. "Am I wrong?"

C.J. dragged her hand through her hair. "No, you're right." A hint of a smile slipped over her lips. "Damn it, I really do hate saying that."

Warrick grinned. "That's just your natural competitiveness coming to the fore." The road stretched unobstructed for the next two miles. He spared her a look. "You know, C.J., just because you grew up in a house full of competitive boys who you were constantly pitting yourself against doesn't mean that everyone is interested in competing with you."

As if they hadn't been in constant competition

from the first moment they were partnered up. "Are you turning over a new leaf?"

"I was never in competition with you." Warrick paused for a moment, then couldn't resist adding, "I was your mentor."

She shifted in her seat to look at him. "I beg your pardon, who was whose mentor?" She was the one with seniority, albeit only by six weeks. In actuality they had grown up together at the Bureau.

"There you go again, competing." A motorcycle policeman was approaching from the opposite direction. Warrick eased back on the accelerator. He glanced in her direction and smiled. It was nice to have her bounce back.

They didn't bother going first to the federal building but instead went directly to her parents' house. Warrick barely had time to stop the car before she was jumping out and hurrying up the walk.

"Remember to open the door, not tear it off its hinges," he called after her.

C.J. ignored him as she fumbled with her keys, then opened the door. Her mother was in the living room. Her father sat in his recliner, holding a fussing baby in his arms.

She crossed to him immediately and took the baby in her arms, breathlessly asking, "How is she? Did she see the doctor? What did the doctor say?"

Behind her, she heard Warrick come in and close the door.

"Dr. DuCane came to her office and saw her,"

her father told her. "She said it would be less costly that way."

"I don't care about the cost. How *is* she?" In time-honored tradition C.J. pressed a kiss to her daughter's forehead to check for a fever. The baby was warm but not burning up the way she'd feared.

"Dr. DuCane prescribed an antibiotic. Your father's already picked it up at the drugstore." Her mother's voice, for once, was calm, soothing. "She has otitis media." C.J. looked at her mother blankly. "Middle ear infection," Diane explained. "You and Wayne were both prone to that when you were little."

C.J. frowned, kissing the baby's forehead again. "She still feels warm."

Diane leaned over and performed her own test. "Her fever's down considerably from late last night. But don't get alarmed if it shoots up again." She spoke from experience. "Children can be sick in the morning, perfectly fine in the afternoon and sick again in the evening."

C.J. sighed. This was a great deal more than she'd thought she'd signed on for initially. Her stomach felt as if it was tied up in knots. "God, when does it stop, Mom?"

"I don't know." Diane laughed softly. "How old are you now?"

C.J. cradled the baby against her. The fussing had lessened a degree. "Point taken."

"You can stay here tonight if you'd like," her mother invited. "I can get your old room ready."

C.J. was sorely tempted by the offer. It would be

easy just to let her mother take over. She was clearly the expert here. But she didn't want to grow dependent on her mother's help. She had to do this on her own.

"Thanks." She addressed both her mother and her father, knowing that he had probably been right there, taking his turn at pacing the floor with the baby. "But I just want to get her home and into her own bed."

"Fine." Diane accepted her daughter's choice. "Then I'll come along with you."

C.J. was torn. There was pride and then there was stupidity. She'd already done one stupid thing in the past twenty-four hours. She wasn't about to go for two. Her protest lacked conviction. "You don't have to do that, Mom."

Diane read between the lines. She'd been a young mother once, too. "Don't worry, I'm not crowding you. I'll just stay long enough to give you an opportunity to shower and change your clothes. You want to get the feel of the road off you, don't you?"

C.J. looked at Warrick significantly. "Yes, I guess that's for the best."

Chapter 11

"You gave me quite a scare there, kidlet."

Finished feeding the baby, C.J. got up from the kitchen table and put the empty bottle on the counter with one hand while she held her daughter close to her with the other. It had been a tough few hours, but, as her mother had promised, things were settling down again. The baby's fever was gone. Thank God.

Walking to the living room, she kissed the top of her baby's head. The soft, fine blond hair brushed against her lips. Not quite ready to put her down for the night, C.J. took her into living room and sat down on the sofa. She needed to give the baby her medicine, anyway.

She looked down at the small face that seemed to watch her with rapt attention. "Of course, I'm new at this, you realize, but I think I might have this panic thing under control.''

C.J. knew better, actually. She had a feeling there would always be an element of underlying panic involved. It was only a matter of how well she hid it when it occurred and how well she performed under its influence.

''Until the next time, probably.'' The baby nestled against her, C.J. unscrewed the top and measured out the prescribed dose on a curved baby teaspoon. ''Now take your medicine like a good girl. The pharmacist told Grandpa it tastes like bubblegum.'' She laughed at that. ''Yeah, right, like you know what bubblegum tastes like. Time enough for that later, when I'm not afraid you're going to swallow it.'' She smiled as the baby's lips parted and she swallowed the medicine without complaint. ''That's a good girl, Joy.''

Then, putting the teaspoon down on the coffee table beside the bottle, C.J. looked at her daughter again and shook her head. She'd been so worried, so scared returning home. How had her mother done it? How had she survived five of them?

''Your grandmother's incredible, cupcake, I hope you know that.'' She rose again, patting the baby on the back. As she started for the stairs, someone rang her doorbell. Perfect timing.

''You expecting anyone?'' she asked the baby. ''It's too late for the Avon lady.'' Setting the baby down in the portacrib she had set up beside the sofa, C.J. made her way to the front door. ''Who is it?''

''Ice-cream man.''

Even through the door, she recognized the voice. C.J. swung open the door. "Warrick? Was there a break in the case?"

"No, no break." He held up the paper bag he was holding. "I just thought you might need one, so I brought you some ice cream."

She looked at him incredulously. "At ten o'clock at night?"

"I stayed late at the office, thought I'd tackle some paperwork for a change." He always put it off as long as he could. It was his least favorite part of the job. Warrick nodded at the car in the driveway. "I see Rodriguez dropped off your car like I asked."

"Yes, he got here about six. Thanks."

"No problem. Are you planning on letting me in anytime soon, or would you rather just lick melted mint chip ice cream straight off your doorstep?"

"Sorry about that." C.J. stepped to the side, letting him pass. "Mint chip, huh?" Grinning, she looked down at the bag and recognized the emblem on the side. He'd bought the ice cream at a place where she and the other Mom Squad members used to congregate after Lamaze classes. C.J. raised her eyes to his. "You stopped at the Ice Cream Parlor?"

"You were always raving about their ice cream, I figured why not." She closed the door behind him. "It was on the way."

The hell it was. "To the opposite side of town."

He frowned, thrusting the bag at her. "Just take it, will you, and stop talking." Warrick crossed to the portacrib and looked down at his special delivery. The baby's eyes had drifted closed. He lowered his voice as he asked, "So how's she doing?"

C.J. was in the kitchen, getting a couple of bowls from the cabinet. "Her fever's down, thank goodness. She's still fussing, but I think the worst is over."

He could hear the relieved smile in her voice. Warrick lingered a moment longer by the portacrib. Funny how something so little could hold on to your heart so tightly, he mused.

He crossed into the kitchen. "I figured I'd see your mother here."

"I sent her home a few hours ago." C.J. scooped out two servings. It hadn't been easy, finally getting her mother to leave. "She left under protest, but I've got to get a handle on this mothering thing on my own." She handed Warrick his bowl, then picked up her own and walked over to the kitchen table. Pulling out a chair, she sat down. "I can't keep depending on her."

"One time doesn't make you hopelessly dependent, C.J." Sampling his portion, he raised his eyebrows in surprise. "Hey, this is good."

She smiled as she slid in another spoonful. "Told you."

Damn but she looked sensual, slipping the spoon between her lips like that. Warrick forced his mind back onto the subject and took another heaping spoonful for good measure.

"You know, accepting help doesn't make you a bad mother—it makes you a rested mother," he pointed out. "Speaking of which, why don't I stick around for a while after we finish our ice cream, maybe let you catch a catnap.''

She knew he probably meant well, but it was still an affront to her capabilities. ''I don't need a catnap, or any other animal nap.''

''Sure you do.'' His grin was wicked as it came into his eyes. ''You didn't exactly get much sleep last night.''

Was he gloating? She couldn't tell. ''Neither did you.''

He inclined his head in agreement. ''Which is why I'm only going to spell you for a few hours.'' He indicated the bowl before her. ''Now eat your ice cream like a good girl and do what I tell you.''

She laughed shortly. ''In your dreams. Since when did you become in charge?''

''The captain is relieved of duty when showing signs of undue stress and/or insanity,'' he recited. ''Sleep deprivation has been known to cause both.'' He polished off his own bowl and debated getting a second serving. ''Now eat, sleep, and I'll take care of the merry.''

''That's eat, *drink* and be merry,'' she corrected. Maybe she should relent a little. Nobody could do everything. ''You're nuts, you know that?'' Her laugh was affectionate.

''I know.'' He pulled the carton over to him and scooped out half a serving more. The serious look in his eyes was at odds with his light tone. ''My partner made me that way.''

Why was it that she could almost feel his words dancing along her skin?

"Okay," she lowered her eyes to her bowl. Communing with green ice cream was a great deal safer right now than looking into Warrick's eyes. "I'll let you stay—but just for a little while."

C.J. looked up from her cluttered desk. Every pile on it represented another possible lead that had to be checked out. Hopefully somewhere was the legitimate tip that would lead them to the killer.

But right now, she was frowning at Warrick. She hadn't seen him when she'd first walked in this morning. He'd pulled phone duty and she'd thought it was best to stay away before someone asked her to do the same.

"You shouldn't have let me sleep that long."

He downed the last of his less than mediocre coffee, then put his mug down on the corner of his desk. "You needed it. Besides, the baby slept right along with you." He was honest about his limitations. "If I'd had to face a dirty diaper, maybe I would have woken you up sooner." He'd left her house at two in the morning to get a few hours of sleep himself before going in to the office. "Feel any better today?"

"Yes. Thanks."

He grinned, digging in again. "Don't mention it."

"I'm also probably five pounds heavier, thanks to the ice cream."

He laughed. "Hey, nobody told you to finish it." His eyes swept over her. "Besides, the five pounds look as if they found a good home. You always were a little too thin."

She arched a brow. "I beg your pardon?"

The assistant director, Edward Alberdeen, picked that moment to walk in, curtailing any further exchange.

"Heads up, people." His booming voice brought everything within the noisy room to a standstill. "Our boy's struck again."

Warrick was the first to reach the A.D. It was a grim fact of life that every new strike meant that much more of a chance that there might be a slip-up, a clue that would finally lead them to their quarry. But the grim reality was that it also meant someone else had died.

"Are we sure it's him this time?" They all knew he was referring to the wild-goose chase he and C.J. had gone on on Saturday. "Lots of people are getting edgy, seeing things that aren't there."

In reply, Alberdeen placed the photograph he'd just received via a colored fax and turned it around so that Warrick, C.J. and the others could all see. The woman in the photograph looked like all the others: blond, a rose clutched in her hands, a cheap pearl choker on her neck to hide the bruising.

"We're sure," he replied grimly. "The M.E. thinks death was within the last twelve hours." He looked down at the photograph, shaking his head. "She's dressed as if she was going to a party."

"Maybe she was. Maybe our killer picked her up and decided to add her to his collection," C.J. suggested. She looked at Alberdeen. "We have a name?"

"Jackie Meyers. Purse wasn't touched, same as

the others. Mother made a positive ID. Here's the address.'' The A.D. handed it to Warrick. ''Go canvass the area, see if we can get lucky this time.'' He said what they'd been saying since the very beginning. ''He's got to slip up sometime.''

''You'd think,'' C.J. muttered under her breath. She looked at the photograph again. It was the face of pure innocence. Just like the other victims had appeared. ''Damn, it's a shame.''

''It's always a shame when someone's murdered,'' Alberdeen interjected. ''You getting anywhere with that theory of yours, Jones?''

She looked back at the piles on her desk. She was going to have to apply good old-fashioned legwork to them soon. With no other strong leads to follow, she'd gone back to her theory that perhaps their killer had been away either in prison or a mental facility somewhere in the county for the past three years and had taken up where he'd left off as soon as he was released. Another possibility was that he might have enlisted. But no other murders matching the killer's MO had turned up anywhere else, so she was less inclined to go that route.

''Not yet. Checking out former inmates is slow work, A.D. Orange County has its fair share of loonies and felons.''

The expression on the A.D.'s long, thin face said that no one had to tell him that. ''Well, keep at it. We don't have much else to go on—yet.''

She nodded, then glanced at the address in Warrick's hand. It wasn't far from where she lived. Had she known the girl, passed her in the mall, perhaps in the supermarket?

The thought of the Sleeping Beauty Killer lurking somewhere close by made C.J.'s blood run cold. Suddenly, she felt too restless to just sit behind a desk. "Okay let's go, boys, and see if we can't catch ourselves a killer."

Warrick gestured toward the door. "You heard the lady, let's roll."

Warrick looked at her as they drove back to the field office. They'd put in a long day, interviewing all the people Jackie Meyers might have interacted with on her last day. A few names had been provided by the girl's mother, and they had gone from there.

The silence got to him. "You're being awfully quiet—again."

She shook her head, as if unaware of her lapse. "I was just thinking how much I hate having to talk to the parents of a victim."

The girl had lived with her widowed mother. The woman broke down twice while talking to them. C.J.'s heart went out to her, but there was nothing she could do. Except catch the killer.

She only hoped that she could.

Warrick slowed down as a late-model Thunderbird merged into his lane in front of them. "Not exactly on my top five list of favorite things, either, C.J." He blew out a breath. The case was getting to all of them. "I wish we'd catch a break."

"Yeah, me, too." She stared out the window, try-

ing desperately to keep her mind focused only on
the case and nothing more. Or, if it drifted in any
direction, that it only settle on thoughts about her
daughter. Anything but on the man sitting beside
her.

She'd made up her mind this morning on the way
to work after she'd dropped off the baby with her
mother that what had happened between her and
Warrick that night outside of Santa Barbara was a
mixture of opportunity, curiosity and, just possibly,
stress. Why else would she have been so vulnerable?
So willing to do something she knew damn well was
a mistake?

Okay, so somewhere in her mind she'd always
wondered what it would be like to be kissed by Warrick, to make love with him.

Now she knew.

Now she could move on.

The hell she could, she thought.

Didn't matter what she felt, what she wanted—
again. She just wasn't going to go there. He was a
box of chocolates and she was on a diet and that's
all there was to that.

Maybe.

Stopping at a light, Warrick glanced at her. "I
never thought I'd say this, but I do miss the sound
of your voice. Talk to me, C.J. Bounce theories off
me. Something. Anything."

She mentally grabbed on to the lifeline he threw
her. That's what this was all about, what it *should*
be about: catching the killer, not about an itch she
couldn't allow herself to scratch again. The last time

she scratched, she was left pregnant and her pride was devastated. She wasn't going to go through that again.

Warrick might not be another Thorndyke, but he wasn't her Prince Charming, either.

She forced her mind back on the case.

C.J. watched the early evening traffic as it went by in both directions. Was the killer in one of these cars? Or was he safely hiding inside his house, waiting for the cover of night before he ventured out to make a move? When would he make a move?

"We're going to be hearing from the crazies again," she finally said. The crazies, well-meaning callers and nut jobs who came out of the woodwork to point fingers in a quest for the limelight, give tips that led nowhere and periodically made confessions that ninety-nine times out of a hundred weren't true. Every crime brought them out in droves.

She and the others had all put in their time on the phones, hoping against hope that the next call would be the one that would lead them somewhere.

"Maybe we'll get lucky," Warrick said, "and Alberdeen'll bring in more people to handle the phones."

She laughed, turning toward him. "You're kidding, right? Alberdeen's a company man. Cost conscious to the ultimate degree. He'll just make everyone work harder until this guy's caught."

"If this guy is caught," he amended.

C.J. frowned. "Damn your pessimism, Warrick. *When,*" she repeated, daring him to contradict her.

Warrick shrugged carelessly. "When," he echoed just to appease her.

He certainly hoped she was right, but odds were not in their favor. They never were. For every crime that was solved, a great many more weren't.

He wished he could stop thinking about C.J. Whenever he wasn't around her, she dominated his thoughts and had ever since they'd slept together last Saturday. The harder he tried to eradicate her from his mind, the less he succeeded.

Sleeping with her hadn't satisfied anything, just as kissing hadn't. It only made him want more. Working alongside of her didn't help matters any, either, but he couldn't very well ask for another partner. If nothing else, it would have been cowardly.

Besides, she was a damn good partner and what she lacked in self-discipline, she more than made up for in tenacity and enthusiasm. He didn't want to work with anyone else. He just didn't want to keep thinking about her *that* way. It was frustrating the hell out of him.

Warrick stopped by her desk. She'd been at it all morning, calling the various people on her lists, narrowing them down as best she could. No one on the outside realized how tedious the work that went into apprehending a killer could be.

He was behind her. She could feel it. It wasn't exactly the way it used to be, when she had almost a sixth sense about her partner. Now it was more.

Now it was driving her crazy.

He flipped a page. "Come up with any good suspects yet?"

Several. None. It all depended on how you looked at it. "I'm winnowing it down to a manageable crowd." She pointed to a clipboard on her desk. "Those I plan to interview face-to-face." She glanced up at him and smiled. "Yeah, I know what you're thinking. Glutton for punishment, that's me."

Especially, she added silently, where he was concerned. They were alone in the office, something that didn't happen very often. She decided to screw up her courage and confront him with what had been nagging at her ever since Sunday. "Why haven't you called me?"

He stared at her. Was she turning all female on him, wanting to know "where this is going" and throw a noose around his neck? "What?"

"You don't drop by to hang out anymore." She didn't want him getting the wrong idea. She just wanted her partner back. If she wanted anything else, that was her problem, not theirs. "My brothers want to know what I did to you."

The word *nothing* was right there, waiting to be set free. But it was a lie. She'd done something to him, all right, he just didn't know exactly what to call it. "Do people still use the word *bedeviled?*"

C.J. cocked her head, determined to keep this light, determined to get back on even keel. "Only if they have long lacy cuffs and wear powdered wigs." She looked at him. "So what do I tell them? My brothers," she prompted when he didn't say anything.

"Tell them the truth. That I've been burning the midnight oil on this case." The case had just taken on major proportions. "It seems the last victim was also the niece of a congressman from Nevada. There's pressure to bring this guy in as soon as possible."

C.J. leaned back in her chair, looking at the screen on her monitor but not really seeing it. She had been toying with a thought for the past two days. Maybe it was time to say it out loud and see how it fared in the light of day.

"Maybe it's not a guy." She could see the skepticism on Warrick's face. "Maybe it's a jealous woman. There *are* female serial killers."

"Not many," he pointed out. He couldn't think of more than a handful. "And she'd have to be strong. All the bodies were moved."

"Not so strong," C.J. countered. She looked at the bulletin board with its photographs of the victims. "Most of the women were small." That fed her theory. "Maybe that's one of the things she has against them. In this image-conscious world, maybe they typify everything she isn't." C.J. shrugged. It was thin, but there was a possibility she could be right. "It might explain the nail polish."

"What, that she's playing house with them? Or beauty parlor?" Warrick shook his head. "I think you're reaching."

She blew out a breath and pushed herself away from the desk. C.J. rose to her feet. Maybe it was time for a break. There was a candy bar in the vending machine with her name on it. "Damn straight

I'm reaching. Reaching for anything I can latch on to, hoping to catch a break."

As she was about to go out the door, Rodriguez stuck his head in. "Guess what?"

"Your fiancée came to her senses and called off the engagement?" Warrick deadpanned behind her.

"Very funny. We think we might have caught a break. Someone just called in saying they remember seeing a car parked in the vicinity where the last body was found. He puts it there around the time the M.E. guessed the victim was killed."

C.J. wasn't biting just yet. "And why would this 'witness' remember that?"

"Because he said he came damn near close to hitting the car. It was half-hidden in the shadows. As a matter of fact, he thinks that maybe he might have scraped a fender."

This was too much to hope for. C.J. tried not to let her enthusiasm go just yet. "This so-called witness wouldn't have by any chance taken down the license plate number, would he?"

Rodriguez grinned. "He did better than that, he took a picture."

C.J. and Warrick exchanged looks. Maybe this *was* too good to be true.

"What?" C.J. cried.

"Why?" Warrick wanted to know.

Rodriguez couldn't wait to tell them. "Listen to this. He said he was burned badly in a minor fender bender once. Hardly tapped the car and the other guy sued him for a hundred grand one day short of a year to the date of the accident. The other guy's car was a wreck and his insurance company wound up dropping him.''

''The point, Rodriguez, the point,'' Warrick prodded impatiently.

''I'm getting to it,'' the other man told him. ''Since then, our witness has been driving around with one of these disposable cameras in his car.''

''Thank God for paranoid people,'' C.J. commented. Taking her purse out, she kicked the drawer shut again. ''Let's go see that witness and get that picture.''

''You don't really think there's anything to this, do you?'' Culpepper had walked in just in time to get the general gist of the story. He looked dubious now.

''Hey, Son of Sam was caught because of unpaid traffic tickets,'' C.J. reminded him. ''Stranger things have happened. Solving a case requires hundreds of hours of dedicated work—and one lucky, totally unrelated break. I hope this is ours.'' She looked at Warrick. ''Wanna join me?''

''As if you could stop me,'' he rejoined, heading out the door right behind her.

''Hey, it was my phone call,'' Rodriguez called after them.

''And we'll see that you get full credit,'' C.J. promised. ''All I want,'' she told Warrick as he pressed for the elevator, ''is this guy's head on a platter.''

''You'll get no argument from me.''

''First time for everything,'' she quipped as she got into the elevator.

Chapter 12

Harry Maxwell was a quiet, soft-spoken man in his midthirties. He lived in a one-bedroom apartment in a run-down building that was situated in the heart of Santa Ana. A trace through the DMV using the photograph of the rear of the vehicle with its license plate supplied by their paranoid witness had led them to Maxwell's door.

After they had identified themselves, Maxwell had hesitantly let them come in. It was clear that the mild-mannered man was not at his best with people. He told them that he liked dogs best. There were three of no particular breed in the apartment that C.J. could see. Possibly more in another room.

He'd led them to his postage-size living room and offered them a seat on his sagging corduroy sofa. Harry perched on the coffee table, the only other furniture in the room besides an old TV mounted on a shipping barrel older than he was.

Small brown eyes bounded back and forth from C.J.'s face to Warrick's as he patiently answered their questions about his vehicle.

He nodded twice at the last question. "Yes, my car was parked by William Mason Park three nights ago. I'm not sure about the time." The admission was made fearfully. "Was that illegal?" His voice was hurried, breathless as he made his apology. "I'm sorry, I stop there all the time. Mostly at night. To think. There's nobody there then. I like it better that way. I won't do it again if it's wrong."

He made C.J. think of someone who had the word *victim* painted in neon colors on his forehead. The kind of man who, when he was a boy, everyone ridiculed. Even the geeks.

Was it an act? Or the truth?

Warrick was incredibly patient as he calmed the man down. "We just want to find out if you saw anyone there that night."

After taking a moment to think, Harry shook his head vigorously. "No. Some ducks, but that's all. Should I stop going there?" he pressed. It was clear that he hoped the answer was no.

C.J. smiled at him kindly. "It might be a good idea to go when the park's open. There's no attendant at night."

At night the gate was closed, but it didn't really offer much of a deterrent. Except for a small three-foot wooden fence around the perimeter, the park was wide-open, easily accessible from the road on foot. Bedford had a low crime rate. People tended to feel safer there.

Until they were killed, C.J. thought.

A shy smile twisted the man's lips as he looked at C.J.. "Thank you. I'll remember that."

C.J. exchanged glances with Warrick, then took out her card. "If you happen to think of anything unusual you might have seen that night after we leave, please give me a call."

He read the card intently. "Yes, ma'am, um, Special Agent..." Harry's voice trailed off as he looked at her hesitantly again, obviously at a loss as to what to call her.

"Agent Jones will do," C.J. told him. She rose to her feet. Warrick followed suit. She nodded at Harry. "Thank you for your time."

C.J. waited until she and Warrick were back inside their own vehicle before turning to him and asking, "What do you think?"

"Could be an act," he allowed. "But right off the top of my head, I'd say he's genuine, which means he's not our guy."

She buckled up as he started up the car. "He looks about as harmless as an anesthetized flea."

There was a break in traffic and Warrick darted in. Someone honked impatiently behind him. He glanced at C.J. "I'm trying to picture that."

If he wasn't their man, then they were back to where they started, wading through the endless phone tips that came in with nothing else to go on. "Never mind, let's just drive back."

The streets in that part of Santa Ana were narrow,

barely allowing enough room for the flow of single-lane traffic and parked cars by the curb. Warrick waited until they were stopped at a light. There seemed to be one every few hundred yards. "So, any news about the christening?"

Father Gannon was still in Ireland. It seemed, miracle of miracles, that his eighty-three-year-old mother had rallied and was on the mend. C.J. had spoken with the secretary, who seemed very hopeful about the priest's pending return. C.J. was keeping her fingers crossed. Father Gannon had been the one to marry her parents and had officiated at all five of their christenings. She was determined that he would baptize her daughter, as well. No one else would do.

"Tentatively it's set for two weeks from Saturday."

Warrick took his foot off the brake. They began inching their way to the next light. "Your daughter's going to be applying to college before she ever gets baptized. Or a middle name." He slanted a quick look at her profile. "You haven't by any chance—"

"No," C.J. snapped, knowing exactly what he was going to ask. "I haven't."

Warrick grinned as he shook his head. "Touchy."

She wasn't touchy, she was desperate. And it wasn't as if she had a clear head and could concentrate on nothing else. There was the added complication of the serial killer they were trying to catch, not to mention that her personal life had been set on its ear because of one fatal slip in a motel room. She was as afraid as ever of getting hurt, but now not quite so sure that she was swearing off all men for life.

C.J. concentrated on the dilemma under discussion. "Look, this is getting worse, not better. Every time I think I have a name, I use it a couple of times and it just doesn't feel right calling her that." She shrugged. He was a man, he wouldn't understand. Men understood very little.

Warrick blew out a breath. "You're making this way more complicated than it is. Names don't have to feel, C.J., they just have to be."

She frowned deeply. Why did she ever think she'd get any support from him? "You're beginning to sound like my mother."

Warrick laughed at the comparison. "I'm not insulted. I like your mother."

"A little support wouldn't hurt, you know."

"I gave you support," he reminded her. "I came over with not one names-for-the-baby book, but two. Any normal person..." His voice trailed off. "Sorry, forgot who I was talking to."

"Very funny. I'll come up with a name and it'll be perfect." She sighed as she looked out the window. They were still going nowhere. In so many ways. "Back to canvassing," she murmured, sliding down a little in her seat. She hated going around in circles, ending up where she'd started.

His sigh was an echo of her own. "Yeah."

C.J. rubbed her temples. Everything was getting blurry.

She'd been at it for the past four hours straight,

staring at screen after screen of inmate names. It felt
as if she was going cross-eyed. This was probably
going to lead nowhere, just like everything else. She
began to doubt the validity of her initial premise,
that the killer had been locked away for three years,
unable to continue his gruesome spree.

Maybe she should just knock it off for the time
being, do something more useful. C.J. started to
close the program when a name caught her eye.

She blinked and looked at it again, then blinked
one more time, almost convinced that she was imag-
ining it. It certainly wouldn't have been the first time
she'd misread a name.

The name remained where it was. In the center of
the list of inmates released from the county jail in
the last six months.

She was afraid to raise her eyes, afraid the name
would disappear. This was too good to be true. Too
good to be a coincidence. "Hey, Warrick?"

"What?"

He realized that he'd snapped the word at her. The
combination of sifting through endless "tips," all of
which had to be investigated before being disre-
garded, and the tension that had all but become a
permanent part of his day had momentarily gotten
the better of him.

He had help with the sifting, everyone on the task
force was taking turns at that. But the tension, well,
that was a whole different matter entirely. That was
his own damn fault.

His and C.J.'s.

He should never have followed through on his

curiosity that night. If you don't know, you don't miss. And he did. Missed the feel of her. Missed making love with her. Missed it a great deal.

Could that kind of thing happen after just one night together?

He didn't think it could, but then, if it couldn't, why did he feel this way? As if he'd been turned inside out and every part of him was aching to have her again. He hadn't even felt this way when he'd slept with his ex-wife the first time.

The memory of his ex-wife threw cold water on his thoughts. Now there was one hell of a mistake, marrying her. His ego wasn't inflated, but he knew he was sharp when it came to working his cases, sharp when it came to picking through clues. But he was hopelessly inept when it came to relationships that didn't involve a Bureau-issued vehicle or weapon.

''Sorry,'' he apologized, running his hand over his forehead. ''Just tired. What have you got?''

She knew she shouldn't allow herself to get carried away, but there had been so many dead ends that the slightest glimmer of something turned into a veritable rainbow of multicolored lights.

She put her finger on the screen, marking her place and looked over toward Warrick. ''Guess who was released five months ago from the county jail?''

''The Easter Bunny, I don't know, C.J. It's a little late to be playing games.'' Despite his less-than-cheerful mood, he got up and came up behind her to see what her sudden burst of excitement was all about.

"Harry Maxwell." She read what was on the screen despite the fact that Warrick was standing behind her and could see for himself. "He was convicted of driving around in a stolen vehicle. Claimed he thought it was his. First-time offense, extenuating circumstances and a little creative lawyering got him a reduced sentence."

"What is it about Maxwell and cars?" Warrick commented. Unlike C.J. he reserved his excitement until they could come up with something more tangible.

"I don't know." She was beaming at him. "But guess how long he was in prison?"

Warrick skimmed down the screen, reading. "Three years."

"Bingo." She swung her chair around to face him. "Give the man a prize."

Because the change in position placed her practically against him, C.J. moved her chair back again. Spears of heat went through her. Stupid time for a carnal reaction, she upbraided herself. She was getting paid to work on the case, not foster the hots for Warrick.

"So, what do we have here?" Warrick reviewed the situation out loud. "A man who's been out of circulation for three years—"

C.J. held up a finger. This was not to be shrugged off. "The length of time that the killings stopped," she emphasized.

"And his car is seen near the vicinity where the body of the last victim was found." He looked at C.J. She knew better. "Circumstantial evidence, nothing more. The grand jury would never indict on this.''

She sighed, deflated. ''I know, I know, we need something else.''

He turned her around to look at him. She had good hunches and he'd learned to listen to them, no matter what he said to the contrary. ''Do you really think that guy's our killer?''

C.J. could tell by his tone that Warrick was highly skeptical. She could see his point, even agree with his point after meeting Maxwell, but something didn't allow her to rule the man out.

''Ted Bundy was gregarious,'' she reminded him. ''Nobody thought he did it, either. And he never fit any profile they came up with for the killer.''

A noise in the doorway had them both looking in that direction. Rodriguez and Culpepper walked in, one more tired looking than the other. They sank down in their respective chairs, both sighing almost simultaneously.

''Where've you been?'' C.J. looked from one man to the other. ''You both look as if someone wiped the floor with you.''

Culpepper grumbled, digging into his pocket for another stick of nicotine gum. ''Alberdeen's got us talking to the families of the victims again, trying to find some kind of link between them other than their looks.''

Warrick moved closer. ''And?''

Rodriguez looked disgusted. ''Still zilch.'' He nodded at C.J. ''He's got us asking questions you should be handling.''

She knew he didn't mean that as an insult, but Rodriguez, like Culpepper, had some very definite ideas about male and female territory. "Like?"

He pulled the top off the soda can he'd brought in with him and drank deeply before answering. "Like where they shopped, what beauty parlor they went to, you know, girl stuff."

C.J. laughed. She could just hear what the two men had to say about the assignment when the A.D. had given it to them. "Consider it an education for when you get married."

"I don't need an education." He drank again, obviously totally parched. "Jane goes to a place called Nina's. I don't like her going because it's not in the best neighborhood, but she raves about it. Wants me to go get my hair styled there, too," he laughed incredulously, running a hand through his mop of curling black hair. "Can you just picture that, me in a place like that? I told her real men don't get their hair styled." He thumped his chest. "Just cut."

"Nina's?" Culpepper echoed, chewing on the name. "Hey, wasn't that the name of the beauty parlor the last victim went to the day she died?" His dull eyes brightened as he looked at his partner. "Her mother said something about her wanting to look her best for that party." He glanced at the bulletin board where the young woman's photograph had been added to the others. "Poor kid."

Warrick suddenly started riffling through his notes. Pads and loose pages began sliding down right and left, some falling on the floor. Culpepper stared at him, puzzled. "What's the matter with you?"

"I've heard that name before." Finding the right set of notes seemed almost impossible. His desk had taken on the appearance of the aftermath of a particularly devastating tornado.

"How?" C.J. pressed, getting up and crossing to his side. Offhand, she didn't remember hearing the name. "One of the people we interviewed?"

"No, one of the victims." He was digging through things with both hands, stopping to read, then discard. "I think she was working there before she was killed." He suddenly remembered the name and went to a different pile. Warrick scanned a couple of notes, then held the spiral pad aloft. "Yeah, here it is. Victim number one. Claire Farrel." He read further. "No, I was wrong, she wasn't working there, she'd quit the week before."

More coincidences? C.J. wondered. But something in her gut told her that they were more than just that. She stood on her toes, trying to read over Warrick's shoulder. The man's handwriting made chicken scratch look like perfect penmanship.

"I give up," she declared, then looked at him for the answer. "Do we know why she quit?"

That wasn't in there. Warrick flipped the pad closed. "Anybody's guess."

Guessing right was the name of the game. For the second time that day, her enthusiasm began to build. She looked at the three men in the room. "How did we miss this before?"

Rodriquez shrugged. "I dunno, it fell through the

cracks, I guess. Probably didn't seem important at the time. Hey, we're only human.''

She nodded. That they were. She tried to think positively. ''What matters is that we found it now.'' She looked at the three men. ''Okay, we've got two victims who went to Nina's. Let's find out if the others went there, too.''

''So what have we got here?'' Culpepper grumbled. His tone indicated that he thought it was all a tempest in a teapot, one of his favorite expressions. ''They were stalked by an irate beautician?''

''We might have a connection,'' C.J. emphasized. ''Who knows where that'll lead us?'' She stopped and looked at the older man. ''You have a better idea?''

''Yeah,'' Warrick cut in, ''instead of pawing through illegible notes, why don't we just go to Nina's and get a client list?''

''Brilliant.'' C.J. already had her purse out of her drawer. She kicked it shut. Culpepper groaned. ''Warrick and I'll go. You two get your beauty rest.'' She turned to her partner. ''Last one to the car's a rotten egg.''

It occurred to him, as he hurried to catch up, that he liked the way her face lit up when she was being enthusiastic about something.

The woman who owned and ran Nina's was a still semi-attractive woman in her midsixties. She gave the impression of having been a knockout when she was younger and behaved as if she still believed that to be true. She'd all but devoured Warrick with her eyes as she listened to him.

C.J. felt as if she might as well not be there, for all the attention the woman was paying to what she had to say.

The owner balked at the idea of producing her client list until Warrick reiterated C.J.'s request. With a surrendering sigh and something about never being able to say no to a good-looking man, the woman pulled up her client list on the antiquated computer.

Warrick sent a less-than-subtle grin toward C.J. before scrolling through the list.

Unwilling to be ignored, Nina sighed loudly. "This is too much, just too much." She rang her hands, careful not to ruin the polish on her long, bloodred nails. "I can't handle any more. First my son, now this."

"Your son?" C.J. echoed.

Warrick raised his eyes from the client list. Every one of the murdered women had come here, at least once, if not repeatedly. They had their connection. Now what did they do with it?

"What about your son?"

C.J. had asked the question, but Nina gave her answer to Warrick. "I just finished paying off the lawyer's fees. Stupid lawyer couldn't even get him free."

Warrick exchanged glances with C.J. "What was he charged with?"

"Some crazy, trumped-up deal. The police claimed he stole a car. My son's not a thief, he's a dear, sweet boy.'' She fluttered her lashes. C.J. struggled to keep from laughing. ''A little slow, maybe, but that doesn't mean someone gets the right to just throw him in jail like that. He used to work here for me, did the shampooing. Sometimes helped with the manicures. The clients all liked him.''

Warrick exchanged looks with C.J. ''What's your son's name?''

Suspicion suddenly entered the carefully made-up eyes. Slim brows gathered over the bridge of her nose. Suddenly she transformed into the protective lioness, fighting for her cub. ''Why, so you can do something to the records and throw him back in? I know how this system works, honey. Always against the little man—''

Exasperated, C.J. looked at the hairstylist closest to her. The woman made no attempt to look as if she wasn't listening to every word of the conversation in the back room. ''You know her son's name?''

''Henry, Herbie, Harry, something like that,'' the woman replied.

C.J.'s eyes darted to the name on the business license. The woman's full name was Nina Maxwell Claymore. Maxwell. *Bingo.* Tapping Warrick, C.J. pointed to the framed sign.

''We'd like a copy of your client list to take with us, please,'' C.J. told the woman.

''And then we'll be out of your hair,'' Warrick added for good measure.

The woman looked uncertainly at them, then with

a huff hit the print button. In the recesses of the back room, a dot matrix printer wheezed to life.

"Still circumstantial, you know," Warrick pointed out as they left the beauty salon.

C.J. finished folding the list and stuck it into her purse. "If you keep tripping over arrows pointing in the same direction, eventually you have to think that maybe that's the direction you should be taking." Opening the door on the passenger side, she got in.

Warrick slid in behind the steering wheel. "You want to try to sell that to a D.A.?"

This was a lot more than they had yesterday. Impatience mingled with a sense of urgency. "So what, we wait until he kills another girl?"

"No," starting the car, he backed out of the small parking lot that Nina's shared with a fortune teller called Madam Alexis, "we catch him in the act and stop him. You have to admit if we get him with a dime-store choker and a rose in his possession, that'll make a stronger case for arresting him."

She crossed her arms before her as he picked up speed. "Don't you ever get tired of being right?"

Warrick grinned. "Hasn't happened yet."

She wished he wouldn't grin like that. It went straight to her gut. The last thing she wanted. C.J. looked out the window. "So what do you want our next move to be? Questioning Harry again? He might break."

"And he might surprise us and not be the guy after all." He turned right at the corner, heading toward the southbound 405 Freeway. "Don't forget, we didn't think it was him after we talked to him."

"*You* didn't think it was him," C.J. emphasized. "I had my doubts."

"Yeah, right."

She didn't particularly care for his smirk. "I did the whole Ted Bundy analogy, remember?"

"Right." It was easier to agree than to argue with her. "Let's see if we can get some surveillance time authorized."

Surveillance, he reflected. That meant the two of them together in cramped quarters for hours at a time. The thought was at once exciting and unsettling. He was just asking for trouble, he realized.

"By the way—" he deliberately tried to keep his tone light "—if Alberdeen authorizes the time, you can't wear your perfume."

"My perfume?" She looked at him in confusion. "Why? What's wrong with my perfume?"

Hands on the wheel, Warrick looked straight ahead. "It's sexy."

"You think it's sexy?"

He could hear the smile in her voice. That probably made her think it gave her some kind of power over him. He shouldn't have said anything.

Too late now.

"Just don't wear it, okay?" he said shortly, switching lanes and speeding up as he made his way onto the freeway.

Chapter 13

Warrick shifted restlessly. His legs were beginning to feel cramped. After three days of fruitless surveillance, all of him was beginning to feel cramped.

C.J. was sitting less than six inches away from him, looking at a bank of monitors. He scowled in her direction. You'd think she'd have a little consideration.

"I thought I specifically asked you not to wear your perfume."

They'd been sitting inside the U-Haul truck parked across the street from Maxwell's apartment building for the past six hours, and the air felt as if it was getting rather scarce. Yesterday it had been a cable truck, the day before, to avoid any undue attention, the truck had borne the insignia of the local electric company.

Maybe it was his imagination, but her perfume seemed to be filling up every available space. It was certainly doing a number on his nervous system.

C.J. didn't bother turning around. "I know."

Maybe this surveillance thing wasn't such a good idea. "Then why did you?"

This time she did turn her stool to face him. What the hell was he talking about? "For your information, I'm not wearing any perfume."

Yeah, right. Did she think he'd lost his sense of smell? "Then what's that scent hovering all through the truck?"

To underscore his point, Warrick leaned over and sniffed her hair. Wildflowers came instantly to mind. A field of wildflowers. With C.J. lying in them, nude, her arms raised toward him.

He backed off, shaking his head. Hopefully shaking out the thought.

C.J. paused, thinking. "That's my shampoo. Or maybe my soap, I don't know." She looked at him. He'd been getting progressively antsier with each hour that went by. "What's the matter with you?"

He looked at her pointedly. Lately, he felt as if his grasp on things was slipping. "I'm not sure."

C.J. put her hand on his forehead, checking for a fever. "Are you coming down with something?"

"I think I'm already down with it." Warrick jerked back his head. It was best if they kept contact down to a minimum. "You don't have to mother me."

"Sorry. Once I'm in the mode, it's hard to stop." Because of the erratic hours she was keeping, the baby was at her mother's. C.J. anticipated coming into an empty house and missed her daughter already. "Maybe you should see a doctor."

He shrugged off her words, turning away from her. He found himself facing a wall of control panels. "A doctor can't help with this."

There was no place to move.

It felt as if the very sides of the truck were closing in, pushing him closer to her. Ever since that night, she'd been on his mind more and more. Like a drug addict who couldn't think of anything else but the source of his addiction and getting just one more hit, he couldn't move his mind far from thoughts of her.

Especially when she was only a reach away.

Warrick moved closer to her almost against his will. Certainly against his common sense. "C.J.?"

There was something in his voice that had her looking away from the monitor that was trained on the building's front entrance.

"What?" The word caught in her throat.

His mind took a coffee break. There was no other way to explain it. Warrick brushed the back of his hand along her cheek, watched as her eyes grew larger. His desire mushroomed.

He lowered his mouth to hers.

The knock on the truck's side panel had them both springing back, startled, two tightly wound coils being released.

C.J. looked at the monitor trained at the rear of the truck and let out a relieved breath. They hadn't been made. She nodded at the sliding door. "It's the B team."

Warrick pulled open the door. Rodriguez and Culpepper climbed in.

"We prefer thinking of ourselves as the A team," Rodriguez informed them. Any available space was all but eaten up. There wasn't enough room left over for a complicated idea.

C.J. looked at the two men who had come to relieve them and deadpanned, "So which one's Mr. T.?"

"Very funny," Culpepper grumbled. He changed places with C.J. and took the stool in front of the monitors. "It's bad enough I've got to trade a warm bed for this." The world outside the van looked fairly dead. "Anything?"

She shook her head. She and Warrick had taken over from yet another team. The two men in the Mustang had followed Maxwell to and from his job as a busboy at a nearby family-style restaurant. "He hasn't left the apartment all night."

"Three days and nothing. I'm beginning to think we're barking up the wrong tree," Rodriguez complained.

He moved past Warrick as best he could, taking his place. Other than a small table, littered with chips, sandwich wrappers and empty containers of mediocre coffee, the inside was dominated by the bank of four monitors, focused on different parts of the building.

There'd been one instance where they thought they'd gotten lucky. Maxwell had left his apartment the first night of the surveillance and driven to Mason Park, the place where the last victim had been found. Unable to follow him without attracting his attention, Warrick had alerted an alternate unit to drive by the area. But when Maxwell got out of his car, his hands were in his pockets, not around a body he was looking to dispose of.

Sneaking past the guard rail, he had made his way to the lake. He walked along its perimeter for almost an hour before returning to his car and driving home again. It appeared that he'd been seeking solitude, just as he'd told them in his statement.

"Give it time." Getting out, Warrick waited for C.J. to join him. "He just satisfied his blood lust. He needs time to work it up again."

"Now there's a comforting thought." With a dramatic sigh, Culpepper closed the van door on them.

The cool air failed to have any effect on him. He still felt warm. Warrick shoved his hands into his pockets, feeling at loose ends. He glanced at C.J. as they headed to the Bureau's car. "You want to go somewhere for a drink or a cup of nonstale coffee?"

She was tempted, but she shook her head. "It's nearly midnight, Warrick. I'd better not."

Both hands on the wheel, he pulled away from the curb. "Right."

Don't say it, don't say it. She might as well have been talking Greek to herself. "But you're welcome to come over if you want a good cup of coffee."

Warrick looked at her, struggling with nobler instincts, instincts that told him this wasn't going to go anywhere so he shouldn't pursue it. He thought of his parents, of his all-but-stillborn marriage. He felt he was a man who didn't know how to love, not by example, not by experience. The best thing he could do for himself, and for C.J., was to call it a night and go home.

He turned the car in the direction of her house. Away from the field office. "Okay."

They both knew it wasn't about coffee.

The house was still when she opened the front door. Just as she'd expected it to be. But the all-pervading loneliness didn't come.

Except for the lamp on in the living room, there was no illumination. Warrick closed the door behind them. "Where's your mother?"

"Home. Her home," she clarified. "With the baby." She tossed her purse on the sofa and led the way to the kitchen. "I thought it would be easier on everyone like that." She smiled ruefully. "Except on me." Reaching in the overhead cabinet for the coffee filters, she laughed softly at herself. "I'm still grappling with separation anxiety, I guess." She flipped open the top and took out a single filter. "I hate being away from her."

He leaned against the counter, watching her. Wanting her. "Then why don't you quit?"

She moved past him, to the refrigerator. The coffee can was on a shelf mounted on the door. "In case you haven't noticed, I'm not exactly independently wealthy. There're bills to pay."

"You've got a law degree," he reminded her. "Your father would be happy to take you into the firm." The man had told him so more than once.

Moving Warrick aside, she opened the drawer he'd been blocking and took out a tablespoon.

"My father would be overjoyed to take me into the firm." She measured out two cups worth of crystals. "It's what he's wanted all along."

He watched her eyes as she spoke. He knew how much her family meant to her. But so did her own self-esteem. "But you wouldn't be happy," he guessed.

"No, I wouldn't." C.J. snapped the plastic lid back on the can. "I'd make a fair lawyer," she judged. "I make a great FBI agent. And I love my work." She returned the can to its rightful place and closed the refrigerator door. "I like catching the bad guys." She turned away from him, measuring out two cups of water and pouring them into the coffee-maker. "Not finding loopholes for them."

He was behind her, so close that all she had to do was take a breath and she would find herself against him. Pinpricks of excitement raced up and down a conveyor belt along her spine.

"What else do you like?"

She could feel his breath on her neck. Everything within her tightened with anticipation. C.J. placed the coffeepot back on the counter and turned around. Her body brushed against his, sending electrical charges between them. She looked up into his face. "Long, slow kisses that go on forever."

He framed her face with his hands and lowered his mouth to hers.

She felt as if he was making love to her just by kissing her lips. Slowly, deeply, until she felt as if she was completely anesthetized. Completely mesmerized. She stood up on her toes trying to draw in ever nuance, every taste, savor every delicious second that their lips were together.

Warrick drew his mouth away and looked at her. Tension tightened around his body, squeezing. Begging for release. "Like that?"

"Just like that," she breathed.

The next moment he swept C.J. into his arms and kissed her again, not so slowly, not so gently. The flame was lit and it traveled through both of them with lightning speed.

C.J.'s arms went around his neck almost of their own volition, her heart pounding. It had been forever since he had made love with her. They had been dancing around each other as if that night in the motel wasn't between them, as if they didn't want this.

They'd both been living a lie.

They both wanted it.

Breathing hard, C.J. moved back, creating just enough space to begin pulling off his clothes.

His movements mimicked hers.

She was making his head spin, his blood pump wildly through his veins. Drawing his head back a fraction, he grinned at her. "I guess this means I have to wait for the coffee."

Damn, if he hadn't started this tonight, she would have. "Shut up and kiss me, Warrick," she ordered.

"Yes, ma'am."

And then the smile faded from his lips as something hot and strong took over. His mind and common sense faded somewhere behind a curtain. All that remained were the needs he'd been grappling with.

He yanked off her bra, her skirt, her blouse was already a casualty. His belly quickened as he felt her hands moving his zipper down the length of him, then stripping away his pants. Her hands felt cool against his flesh, hardening him even further.

Warrick kicked his pants aside, separating their bodies just long enough to throw his shirt off his arms. The next heartbeat he was holding her against him again, his hands traveling along the length of her, making her his, everywhere he touched. Everywhere he promised to touch.

Now. She wanted him now…inside of her, filling her. Making her think of nothing else, no serial killers, no responsibilities, no fears.

Just Warrick.

Just him.

C.J. felt almost feral in his arms. She wanted him to feel as wild as she did at this very moment.

Her mouth traveled along his mouth, his neck, his ear. Branding him. Driving him out of his head.

It took everything he had not to throw her on the floor, to take her here, this moment. But that would be too soon, too quick. That would be placing his own pleasure above hers, and he wanted to pleasure her. Because seeing her twist and turn beneath his lips, wanting him, wanting more, heightened his own excitement beyond measure.

Locked in a heated embrace, C.J. wound her legs around his torso. Desire surged. She could feel herself moistening, wanting him. The next moment she felt herself being lowered onto the kitchen table.

C.J. could barely swallow. The throbbing pulse in her throat wouldn't let her.

Trying to draw air into her lungs, she moved her head away from him. "It's too late for dinner," she whispered.

His eyes were dark with longing as he looked at her. There was only a hint of a teasing smile on his lips. "But not for a feast."

Before she could ask him what he meant, Warrick showed her.

His mouth worked along her body, tempting, teasing, leaving his mark damply on every inch he passed. C.J. arched her body against his lips, tiny explosions beginning to take hold along her skin, within the very center of her.

Her need for him grew to astronomical proportions. She reached for him, but he gently, firmly, moved her hands away, all the while continuing the long, sensual journey along her body.

His tongue trailed along her belly, making it quiver in anticipation. She felt herself ripening for him to the point that she didn't think she could stand it a moment longer.

And then, after anointing each thigh in slow, moist strokes, he found the very core of her.

C.J. moaned something almost unintelligible, her body separating from her mind as an avalanche of sensations thundered all through her.

First one wave hit and then another. She felt like

a wild animal, glorying in the pleasure, but wanting him to be with her.

Summoning strength from some nether region, C.J. drew herself up, pushing him away just far enough to be able to slide her legs back around his torso.

She pulled him to her, teasing him with her body, her invitation clear. Her mouth sealed to his.

The next moment she was flat against the table again with Warrick looming over her, like a lord over a slave.

But this wasn't about control, about power. It was only about pleasure. About giving.

"Now."

It was half an order, half a plea, the single word dragged along her raw throat.

She thought she heard him murmur, "Yes, ma'am." Thought she felt his smile against her skin, but she wasn't sure. All she knew was that she wanted him. Despite the climaxes he had given her, she wanted him, wanted to join with him the way it was always meant to be.

Wanted Warrick to feel the jarring power the way she had.

This time, when he entered her, she was the one who initiated the rhythm. At least the first step. The rest of the dance he led, taking her with him every step of the way.

Her breathing became erratic, or maybe she stopped breathing altogether. She wasn't sure.

Nothing mattered except climbing up to the summit together.

And then the explosion reached her, shaking her body. She dug her nails into his back, glorying in the feel of him, in the moment they shared, her heart hammering so hard she was certain it would take a team of cardiac surgeons to return it to its rightful place.

She didn't care.

C.J. kept her eyes closed, lost in the swirls of sensations that were settling all over her. Lost in the feel of him, of the length of his body covering hers.

How was he managing that without crushing her?

She opened her eyes and realized that he was raised on his elbows, balancing his weight, looking down into her face.

He kissed her lips softly.

She almost felt shy. How was that possible? What was he doing to her? She felt as if she'd been turned inside out and then back again.

And wanted more.

"Definitely more stimulating than coffee," he whispered against her ear.

The next moment he was rising up, then getting off the table. He took her hand, helping her up.

C.J. felt a little woozy as she sat up. She must have swayed, because she felt his arms closing around her protectively. She loved the feel of his hard chest against her.

"You okay?"

She nodded, or thought she did. C.J. put her hand to her head, as if that would still the room and put the world back into focus.

"Just a little adrenaline rush. I think the blood

totally drained out of my head.'' Taking a deep breath, she hopped off the table. He drew her to him, closing his arms around her. C.J. leaned her cheek against him. She felt safe, protected. Happy. She looked at the table. ''You realize, of course, that I'm going to have to burn that now.''

He tilted her head back a little, smiling into her eyes. ''Funny, I was thinking of having it bronzed, myself.''

''A trophy?''

That sounded much too harsh, much too cold. Neither had any place here. ''A keepsake,'' he corrected.

It was a silly word. But it still managed to warm her heart.

The next moment she felt herself being swept off the floor and up into his arms. ''I'd like to see your bedroom now.''

She'd half expected him to say something about the hour and needing to get home. C.J. smiled as she laced her arms around his neck. ''First door to your right.''

''And straight out to morning.''

''What?''

''Nothing, just paraphrasing Peter Pan's flight plan to Neverland.''

Never. The word she'd used when thinking of falling in love. Never. The word that didn't work anymore. Nerves moved through her, cautioning her not to say anything. Not to ruin the moment. Not to expect what couldn't be.

"Are you planning on flying tonight?" she asked as he took the stairs.

Warrick brushed a kiss against her hair. "I already have. But the plane isn't grounded yet."

"Big words," she teased.

He came to the landing. "I never say anything I don't mean."

He stared at the house.

They were inside. Claire and that man. He'd seen them walk in. He'd sneaked out of his apartment, using his secret route through the old basement that linked to the next house.

No one saw him.

But he saw them. Saw them watching him.

Tag, they were it.

But he didn't have time to play. Not now, not when everything inside him hurt so bad.

She was doing it again, just like the last time. She was giving herself to someone else when she should have been his. Would have been his.

He had to claim her again, just as he had the last time. And the time before that.

He needed to save her. Before she became any more spoiled.

He settled into the shadows of the greenbelt, watching the house. His fingers rubbed the pearls on the necklace in his pocket.

Chapter 14

As the mists of contentment began to fade away, Warrick slowly became aware of something else hovering in the recesses of his mind. A small, nagging sensation that had been steadily nibbling away at him, taking tiny bites out of the fabric of his resolve with sharp, steely teeth.

He recognized it for what it was. Fear.

Not the kind of energizing fear that accompanied him into darkened alleys, stood beside him in confrontations with thieves and killers who could end life as he knew it in the blink of an eye if he so much as let a fraction of his guard down. That fear helped keep him alive.

This fear ate away at the lining of his stomach.

This fear had to do with C.J. And what she was doing to his world.

It was as if, no matter how alert he was, he had no control, no say over what was happening to him. He didn't like it. It made him uneasy. At any moment his life could go completely out of kilter.

How had he let that happen?

She could sense the change in him.

C.J. turned her head, her cheek brushing along his bare chest, sending delicious little shock waves through her body. There was a pensive look in his eyes. "What are you thinking about?"

Warrick couldn't tell her. Couldn't give voice to his thoughts. Maybe he should have, maybe saying his fears out loud would dissolve them like ghosts in the night, but that wasn't his way. He'd learned early on to work things out for himself. Now was no different.

Besides, she was the problem, so how could he tell her what was on his mind? Simple, he couldn't. Since she was waiting for him to say something, he lied. There was nothing else he could do.

"Just that the christening's this Saturday—" He lowered his glance to her face. "It is this Saturday, isn't it?"

After all the postponements, she didn't blame him for being sarcastic. "Yes, it's this Saturday. Father Gannon's back, his calendar's clear, and there don't appear to be any emergencies in the making, so I feel pretty safe in saying that there's nothing to get in the way."

He played with a strand of her hair, sifting it through his fingers, wondering how he could go back to life as it had been. Feeling that he couldn't. "Have you come up with a middle name yet?"

She sighed mightily, staring off at the ceiling. Feeling his eyes on her. "No."

"That's okay, she doesn't need a middle name."

In her present vulnerable state, defensiveness seemed second nature to her. "Yes, she does."

"Then come up with one." It sounded almost like an order. He knew his patience was short, not because of her inability to come up with some name no one would ever use, but because of the turmoil going on inside him.

Why was he snapping at her? "Don't you think I would if I could? I told you, this is important to me. To her." C.J. sighed. She'd fallen asleep twice this week with the baby book opened to one page or another. "I have to find just the right name."

He'd never seen anyone have so much trouble with a name. "You're not thinking of postponing the christening, are you?"

"No." C.J. ran her hand over her forehead. She could feel a headache in the making. "I don't know what I'm going to do."

"Just pick a name, any name." It shouldn't be so hard. He locked his fingers together, holding her to him. "If you find one you like better, you can always have it legally changed."

She sat up and looked at him. "I can't do that. That'll mess with her mind."

He blew out a breath, thinking for a moment. "Tell you what, I'll put the five top contenders in a hat and just pick one."

Because she was more than a little afraid that she had emotionally abdicated control over her life to him, she was immediately on her guard, taking offense. "Why do you get to do it?"

She was nitpicking. "Fine, you do it." Made no difference to him, he thought. "Have your mother do it. Have the bag boy at the grocery store do it. It doesn't matter who does it, C.J. It doesn't even matter if she *has* a middle name, except to you. Stop obsessing and just pick one. It shouldn't be this hard."

There was no point in bristling. "You're right, it shouldn't be," C.J. relented. "I guess it's this case, it has me completely preoccupied."

As if to prove her wrong, Warrick ran his hand along the swell of her body. She could feel a small wave of heat following the path he'd created.

"Okay, maybe not completely," she allowed. "But it's on my mind almost every waking minute." With a frustrated sigh, she curled into him, resting her head on his chest. The wheels in her brain began to turn. "This investigation's not going anywhere. It could be weeks before Maxwell zeroes in on anyone. Just because we think he killed two women in a short time frame doesn't mean he'll do it again."

He'd worked with her long enough to know she was going somewhere with this. Warrick stopped stroking her hair. "So what are you saying?"

She hesitated for a second, looking for the right words. "Why don't we set a trap for him? We know where he works. I can show up there, really get into his line of vision. Find a way to talk to him, get him to fixate on me.'' She raised her head to look at him, becoming enthusiastic. ''After all, I more than fit the general description of women he seeks out.''

Was she out of her mind? ''No.''

He'd all but fired the word at her point-blank. She stared at him, dumbfounded. ''What do you mean, 'No'?''

Why did she have to challenge everything? ''It's a two-letter word, what's so hard about it? No. As in no, it's a dumb idea. And I want you to drop it.''

She didn't like being dismissed out of hand like this. ''You have any better ones?''

''Yes,'' he answered evenly, ''we continue the surveillance.''

C.J. frowned. This wasn't like him. He knew as well as she did why this wouldn't work. ''We can't continue it indefinitely, and it could be weeks or months before Maxwell does anything, we don't know. He doesn't have a pattern—we've already established that. Besides, we're on a day-to-day basis as it is. Alberdeen can pull the plug on surveillance anytime.''

''Then Alberdeen'll come up with another idea,'' he snapped at her. ''You're not going to dangle yourself in front of a serial killer like so much bait on a damn hook, C.J., and that's that.''

Her eyes widened. He'd never treated her like this before. ''Since when did you get the right to make decisions for me?''

''Since now,'' he said tersely. Since she'd messed with his mind and turned his world inside out. Since he'd started thinking of her as something other than his partner.

He was acting territorial, and if he thought she was going to put up with it, he was sorely mistaken. "Just because we're sleeping together doesn't give you the right to interfere in my life."

"Interfere?" She made him sound like some kind of doorstop. "Is that what it is?"

She'd wounded him and she knew it. That hadn't been her intent. She just wanted him to see reason. It *had* to be this way. "It is when you start telling me what I can or can't do, yes."

"Well then, maybe we shouldn't be sleeping together." He threw off the covers and got up. Warrick kept his back to her as he started to put on the clothes they'd brought upstairs earlier. "Maybe this whole thing was a mistake." He could feel his anger flaring out of control. Just as his emotions had. It had something to do with reflexes and self preservation. "You know, that's what it was. A mistake. And I made it—" he pulled on his pants "—thinking that this would work."

"A mistake?" she echoed, staring at his back. The word couldn't have cut into her more than if it had been placed on the edge of an arrow and fired directly into her heart.

In a huff she pulled on her sweater and her jeans, foregoing any underclothing. She wasn't about to be naked when he was dressed to the teeth. It made her feel much too vulnerable and she'd exposed herself far too much already.

Warrick left his shirt unbuttoned as he tucked it

into the waistband of his pants. He was furious with her for the foolish risks she wanted to take, furious with himself for caring so much that he felt his emotions going out of control.

This was what he got for letting his guard down. He'd given her this power over him. What had he been thinking?

Damn it, hadn't he known this wasn't going to work? He knew he was no good at male-female relationships. How had he let this go so far, allowed it to affect him so deeply?

"Yeah, a mistake," he snapped back. "Neither one of us has a great track record when it comes to relationships. That should have given us a clue that this was all wrong." He blamed himself most of all. "I, at least, should have seen it coming."

What was he saying? That she was too stupid to learn from her mistakes? The headache grew, tangling her thoughts with her emotions, making everything murky, everything painful. "And you don't think I should have?"

Jamming his feet into his shoes, he got up and headed for the hall. "You've got your head up in the clouds so many times, I'm surprised you don't periodically fall off the sidewalk."

She followed him out, stifling the urge to pummel his back with her fists. Not knowing how they got to this point. "If I did, it would be because I was tripping over you. You always see the dark side of everything, always refuse to even entertain the idea of letting a little sunlight in."

He swung around to look at her. "What the hell
are you talking about?"

"I don't know." And she didn't. Everything felt
confused. But he'd hurt her and she wanted to lash
out. "Just get out."

He turned away from her and crossed to the stairs.
"That's what I'm doing. As fast as I can."

"Not fast enough to satisfy me."

But even as he headed down the stairs, she went
after him, stunned, appalled. Watching everything
unfold before her like some kind of disaster she was
unable to stop. Something was making her egg him
on, grasping at the excuse, at straws.

Anything to make him leave.

Because to have him stay was too frightening.

She'd seen the vulnerable side of herself and she
didn't like it, didn't want it. He made her weak because he made her want.

He had to go.

"And you can forget about this Saturday," she
shouted at him. Warrick glared at her over his shoulder as he yanked open the door. "I'll get one of my
brothers to be the baby's godfather. I don't want to
have someone like you in her life."

"Fine with me." He slammed the door.

She jerked it open. "You don't get to slam the
door in my house," she shouted at Warrick's re-
treating back. "I do!"

And she did. She slammed it as hard as she could.
Then sank down against the door and started to cry
huge, body-shaking, soul-racking sobs.

She wasn't sure just how long she sat there on

the floor, her arms wrapped around her knees, her face buried against them.

Long enough to cry herself out.

She felt exhausted. Numb. Rising to her feet, C.J. tried to think, to pull her thoughts together out of the quagmire they'd descended into.

She dragged her hand through her hair. She felt shell-shocked. What the hell had just happened here?

Putting one foot in front of the other, she made it to the small powder room just off the foyer.

This is what she got for letting herself fall in love again. No, not again, this had been something different from what she'd felt for Tom. When she'd loved him, she hadn't lost a part of herself. She had this time. Warrick had taken out a piece of her soul. And then he'd twisted her inside out until she didn't know which way was up.

Who the hell did he think he was, telling her what to do?

He was the man she was in love with, that's who. And that had been *her* big mistake.

Damn it, what was wrong with her? How could she have let something like this happen?

But that was just it, she hadn't ''let'' it happen, it just had.

The feelings for Warrick had been there all along. All they had needed was the right catalyst to be set free. He'd kissed her, and suddenly all those feelings made a run for the border, a break for freedom.

And look where that had gotten her. Miserable in

a semidark house, carrying on futile arguments in the recesses of her mind.

"You would have thought you'd have learned after Tom," she said to the tear-stained face staring back at her in the mirror. "What would it take for you to realize that you aren't going to find the kind of thing your parents have...that relationships like theirs are the exception, not the rule?"

C.J. realized she was shouting at herself. "Oh, great, now I'm going crazy. Perfect, just perfect."

Trying to pull herself together, she splashed cold water on her face, hoping that would somehow wash away all the unwanted emotions that were running rampant through her.

She was not about to allow Byron Warrick to have control over her, to affect her this way. They had made love, so what? Not even love, she amended silently, they'd had sex. That was it, pure and simple. Nothing more, just sex.

A sad smile curved her lips.

Who was she kidding? Maybe it had been "just sex" to him but not to her, she thought miserably. To her it had been something more, something special.

Too bad. It hadn't been to him, and it took two to make a decent relationship. She'd learned that much from Tom. Time to pick up the pieces and move on.

She realized that she'd wandered into the kitchen. The coffee was still in the filter inside the coffee-maker, where they'd left it. Untouched.

She debated for a minute, then shrugged. What

the hell, she wasn't going to get any sleep tonight, anyway. Maybe she'd have a cup of coffee and call Culpepper to see if there'd been any new developments.

C.J. placed the glass coffeepot under the spout and hit the on button. Grumbling noises slowly filled the stillness around her.

She could feel tears forming again. She needed noise, music, something to fill the awful void she felt inside of her. C.J. switched on the radio on the counter.

A mournful tune greeted her. Swallowing choice words, C.J. switched the radio off again rather than hunt for another station. With her luck, every station would be playing a sad song about love that had gone wrong.

She didn't need music, she told herself. What she needed to do was concentrate on the case.

The hell with what Warrick thought. As far as she was concerned, she'd come up with a damn good plan. It was a whole lot better than waiting for the Sleeping Beauty Killer to try to do away with another innocent, unsuspecting woman. Even with the task force waiting in the wings to protect her, the next would-be victim would undoubtedly be traumatized by her contact with the serial killer.

But not her.

Her nerves were stronger than that. This was what she was paid to do. The only thing that traumatized her were special agents who didn't turn out to be so special after all.

She picked up the phone and punched the buttons

on the keyboard with the number to Culpepper's cell phone. He answered after two rings.

"Hi, it's Jones. Anything?"

"What's the matter, C.J., you can't sleep?" Culpepper guessed. "Try coming back here. Watching the monitors'll put you right out. It's dead as a doornail outside. It looks like Maxwell's tucked in for the night. Sure wish I was."

She nodded. No escape for her there. "Call me if anything changes."

"Other than a cat wandering down the street?"

She laughed shortly. "Other than that."

"You got it. Now go to bed, Jones, or come here and spell me because I could use the sleep."

"G'night, Culpepper." She replaced the receiver and turned to the coffeemaker.

Clearing off the counter, she opened the cabinet below the sink to throw the crumpled napkin away. The garbage pail was full to overflowing. She thought of just leaving it, but this time of year it was an open invitation to ants. With a sigh she tied up the white garbage bag and pulled it out of the pail.

She went out to the side of the house where the garbage containers were kept. She threw the bag into the largest one, then turned to go back inside.

Her head jerked up. She thought she'd heard something.

Listening, she couldn't make anything out. Probably just the neighbor's cat, running through the bushes. With a shrug she went to her door. Opening it, she was almost across the threshold when someone came up behind her and bumped into her.

Caught off guard, C.J. stumbled into her living room. She swung around, arms raised defensively in front of her.

Harry Maxwell was standing inside her house.

Chapter 15

Warrick glared into the night, struggling to rein in his anger as he drove down the quiet streets. The windows of his car were down. The air fought a duel as it rushed in on both sides of him, pushing his hair into his eyes. He hardly noticed.

He flew past a light that was about to turn red, barely squeaking through.

Damn it, he'd let her get to him. He'd known better, and yet he'd let her get to him.

His knuckles tightened on the steering wheel as he beat another light before it turned red.

He should never have let any of this happen. Should have stopped it before it ever started. He wasn't a novice at this sort of thing. That first kiss should have warned him that he was on dangerous ground and that it would only get worse.

But that first kiss had stirred him just enough to make him want more.

Well, he'd gotten more, a hell of a lot more than he bargained for, and the whole thing had just blown up in his face.

Warrick shook his head. Half an hour ago he'd been in bed with C.J., feeling utterly invulnerable, and now he was driving home, angry and at a complete loss as to what had happened back there, other than the fact that C.J. had gone off like a Roman candle at a Fourth of July display.

His timing off, Warrick was five feet away from the crosswalk as the light began to turn red. He thought of racing through it. There was no traffic in either direction. At this hour the streets of Bedford were deserted. Shrugging, he eased back on the gas pedal and came to a stop just over the line.

Any way he sliced it, C.J. had a hell of a lot of explaining to do.

He let out a long, measured breath, waging a silent battle in his head. He'd always moved on when things turned sour. No reason to change his mode of operation this late in the game. He was just going to go straight home and forget about everything, put all of this behind him.

When the light turned green, he made a U-turn.

C.J.'s heart started to race as she stared at the stooped man before her. There were smudges of soot or something black on his beige shirt and across one cheek.

What was he doing here? How had he gotten past

Culpepper and Rodriguez and the surveillance cameras? Wouldn't they have seen him? But Culpepper had just told her everything was quiet.

Were there two of Maxwell, a twin they didn't know about?

C.J. told herself to remain calm. "Hello." She smiled warmly at him.

Harry was fidgeting with the edge of his sweater with one hand. He was holding a single long-stemmed red rose in the other.

C.J.'s breath hitched in her throat.

"Is it too late?" Harry asked hesitantly, his eyes fastened on the tips of his run-down loafers. "Because I can come back if it's too late."

Adrenaline was rushing through her veins. She forced herself to tear her eyes away from the rose. She wasn't going to catch this man by being afraid.

"No, it's not too late." Her voice was deliberately soft, coaxing. She wanted him off his guard. "Did you want to tell me something, Harry?"

At the mention of his given name, Maxwell looked up shyly, an almost bashful smile playing on his lips. "I like it when you call me Harry."

"That's your name, isn't it? Harry. Harry Maxwell." More like Harry Houdini, she thought, if he could elude both the surveillance team and the cameras.

Harry nodded his head like a child eager to answer a question right, eager to please the teacher.

The rose made her uneasy. Had he come to kill her? But he seemed so guileless, so uncertain of himself. Could he really be a serial killer?

She forced herself not to look over her shoulder. Her weapon was on the side table, but she felt fairly confident that she could get to it in time if she needed to. Still, she wished she was wearing her spare, the small pistol she kept strapped to the inside of her thigh.

Well, she'd wanted to play bait. This was her chance. "Would you like to come in, Harry?"

He nodded again, his hair bobbing into his face. He pushed it away nervously. C.J. stepped back, opening the door farther, her smile inviting.

Harry moved across the threshold as if an invisible hand was tugging on his sleeve, leading him inside. He looked around like a tourist at a national shrine, taking it all in reverently.

"This is nice."

"Thank you." She eased the door closed, glancing out into the street. She would have felt a great deal better if she could have spotted a squad car, or one of their own vehicles. But the street was deserted.

"You've changed some things."

The comment caught her off guard. C.J. turned away from the door and tried not to stare at him. Had Maxwell been in here before? When she wasn't at home? She struggled not to shiver at the thought. It gave her the creeps.

"A little," she answered evasively. If he was the killer, maybe he was confusing her with one of the women he'd killed. C.J. was careful to keep some room between them. "Do you like it?"

He nodded, then turned to her. The rose was

pointing toward the floor. "You've been watching me."

Oh damn, she thought. He suspected. Was that why he was here? Was this all just an act?

"You don't think I notice, but I do," he was saying. "I notice you watching me. I've been watching you watching me. That's why I used the old route to get here."

"The old route?" She didn't understand. Was this some ritual he was referring to?

Maxwell nodded. He drifted about the room, smoke looking for somewhere to settle, leaving a trail in its wake. She moved with him, always wary that he could turn suddenly.

"Through the basement. I found a tunnel there. It goes to the other building. The one I used to live in with my mother before I went away."

Was he referring to being sent to prison? Or when his mother had married his stepfather and they'd moved to another city? She never took her eyes off him.

"I use that when I don't want anyone watching me."

They needed something more than circumstantial evidence and gut hunches. She needed to get him to say something incriminating.

C.J. took a step closer to him. Friend, confidante. "Why don't you want anyone watching you?"

"Because it's a secret. The way I feel about you, Claire," he told her breathlessly, then added, "I can't tell anyone."

Claire, he'd called her Claire. Who was Claire?

C.J.'s mind raced, trying to recall the names of all the victims. Wasn't one of them named Claire?

And then she remembered. The first victim's name had been Claire. In his mind was he killing the woman over and over again for some transgression?

"Why can't you tell anyone?" she coaxed.

He began to fidget again, as if to avoid something. "Because they'd laugh at me." Maxwell raised his eyes to her face. They were filled with pain. "Like you did."

Damn, he almost had her going. *He* was coming across like the victim, not the women he killed. "When, Harry, when did I laugh at you?"

"The first time." His eyes were sad as he looked at her. He made her think of a stray puppy. A very dangerous stray puppy, she reminded herself. "When I followed you home from my mother's shop." His face clouded at the memory. "I had to get you to stop laughing."

Okay, we're going for the jackpot here. "How, Harry, how did you get me to stop laughing?"

He looked at her in confusion. "You know how, Claire." He looked down at his hands as if they were a thing apart from him. "I put my hands where the sound was coming from." As he spoke, he seemed to be reliving the moment, his voice getting more agitated. "I could feel it under my fingers. Coming up. Hurting me. So I squeezed it." He looked at her again. "I squeezed until you stopped laughing. And then you were so still." He smiled the same shy smile. But this time it seemed eerie to her. "You looked like you were sleeping. And then you were mine. Just mine. He couldn't have you anymore."

There was more to this? An accomplice, maybe? "He?"

"That guy you were with." Anger contorted his face, looking strangely out of place. "The one who kept touching you." His eyes darkened as he looked at her accusingly. "He's back again, isn't he? He looks different, but he's back. Touching you. Don't deny it. I saw him." He took a step toward her, squaring his shoulders. It was the first time she realized that he was taller than she was. "He can't have you. You belong to me." Agitated, Maxwell was yelling now.

She had to placate him until she could reach her gun, C.J. thought. She'd allowed him to lead her away from the weapon.

Her tone was soft, compliant. "Okay. I belong to you. Just you."

He shook his head stubbornly, like a child refusing to be lied to.

"No, you say that now, but I know you. You'll see him again." He was breathing hard now, struggling with a rage that colored his face. "I don't want you to. It hurts to see you with him like that. You never look at me like that."

She licked her lips, stalling for time. Trying to play up to him. "Like what?"

"Like you love me," he pouted.

Because she was trying to calm him, to lull him

into a false sense of security, she took a step closer to him. "But I do, Harry, I do love you."

He shook his head again. Maxwell was clutching the rose so hard he was bending the stem. She saw it drooping.

"That's what your mouth says, but not your eyes."

"That's not true, Harry," C.J. protested with feeling.

It only seemed to anger him more. "Don't lie to me! You want me to go," he guessed. "But don't you see, I can't go? I love you. I just want to be close to you. To touch you."

He combed his fingers awkwardly through her hair. C.J. held herself perfectly still. He was as dangerous as a bear invading a campsite.

His eyes seemed to bore into her. "You're afraid of me. Why are you afraid of me?" He dropped his hand to his side. "I won't hurt you, Claire. It won't hurt, I promise."

Her heart began to hammer. He *had* come to kill her. "What won't hurt?" she prodded. "What are you going to do to me, Harry?"

"Make you mine again. See, I brought you a present." Digging into his coat pocket, he pulled something out and held it up for her to look at.

It was a cheap, imitation pearl choker. The same kind that the others had on.

Bingo.

He beamed at it proudly. "People say I don't think. My mother says I don't think. But I do. I think of everything." He dangled the necklace before her, eager for her approval. "This is so no one'll see."

Her mouth was so dry, she thought she was going to choke. But she had to keep him talking, had to get him to say he killed the others.

"See what?"

Her questions seemed to be annoying him. "How I made you mine."

"You mean the bruises?"

He frowned. "No bruises. You'll be perfect." And then he looked at her hands. "You bite your nails." He beamed proudly. "I can fix that. I'll make them pretty. Just like you."

C.J. took a step back. One more step and she could pivot and lunge for her gun.

Maxwell saw her looking toward the weapon. His breath shortened and was audible as anger came. "No, you can't have that, Claire. You can't hurt me with that, I won't let you."

Okay, maybe a little verbal shock treatment would work here. "I'm not Claire, Harry. I'm Chris. You killed Claire."

There was horror in his eyes. "No, no, I didn't. *You're* Claire, my Claire."

"We can get help for you, Harry. Your mother's very worried about you." She saw rage in his eyes at the mention of his mother. So much for thinking that all serial killers hating their mothers was a load of garbage. Maxwell clearly detested his. "*I'm* very worried about you." She put her hand on top of his. "Won't you let me help you?"

He jerked his hand away. "I don't want help, I want you. Forever. This time it'll be forever."

When she tried to turn away, Maxwell grabbed her by the wrist, his fingers closing around it like a vise. He was a great deal stronger than he appeared.

The sound of breaking glass coming from the back of the house made him jump. It was all the distraction she needed. C.J. yanked her hand out of his grasp and ran for her weapon.

The next second, searing pain shot through her scalp. Maxwell had grabbed her by her hair. He pulled her to him roughly. "No!"

He looked crazy, she thought. Was this the face the victims saw before they died? "Harry—"

"No, you can't scream." He shook his head from side to side, adamant. "You can't. They'll hear you. Everyone'll hear you."

He released her hair only to grab her by the throat. And then both hands were around it, squeezing, stealing her air. C.J. clawed at his fingers, trying to pull them away, but he wouldn't release his hold.

"Let her go, Maxwell!" Warrick roared. His weapon was trained on the other man.

Warrick. C.J. couldn't even cry out his name. Her windpipe was closing.

Harry looked at him as if Warrick had just told him to do something that was beyond his scope.

"I can't. She won't be mine if I let go. She'll be yours." He squeezed harder. "You can't love her like I do."

Panic seized Warrick. Maxwell wasn't going to let her go. He was going to kill her. Warrick cocked his weapon. "Yes, I can, Maxwell. I do. I love her more than you. Now let her go or I'll shoot!"

But Harry shook his head again, squeezing harder.

The air was gone from her lungs, from her body. There was nothing left to draw on. Her head was spinning, the room was darkening.

She thought she heard an explosion just before she hit the floor.

She blacked out for one terrible second. And then there was air, sweet air and she was gasping, coughing, trying to suck it all into her lungs.

She thought she heard Warrick's voice yelling, saying something about "agent down" and needing "immediate assistance." There were more words. Garbled, they floated through her head, mixing with shooting lights. She heard him say "ambulance."

Still gasping, her chest heaving, C.J. realized that her eyes were shut.

Prying the lids opened, she saw Warrick looking down at her. She was on the floor and he was cradling her against him.

She'd never seen him look so worried before, not even the night she gave birth to her baby.

He saw her eyes flutter. His heart echoed the movement. He'd just been to hell and back in the space of an eternal minute.

He hugged her to him. "Oh, God, C.J., are you all right?"

C.J. struggled to sit up. She ran her fingers tentatively over her throat. It ached something awful. She could still feel Harry's fingers, pressing the life out of her.

Trying to swallow, she coughed, then nodded. "Yes." The word came out in a gasp. She tried again after a beat. "But I think my concert-singing career is over."

He rocked back on his heels. "Damn it, C.J., you scared the hell out of me." Shouting at her, Warrick offered up a silent prayer of thanksgiving. "I thought you were dead."

"That makes two of us."

Shakily she tried to gain her feet and almost fell. Warrick rose quickly and helped her up. It was then she saw Harry on the floor, blood pooling beneath him. Her breath caught.

"Is he—"

"No, just knocked out." He'd already checked for a pulse. "I hit him in the shoulder." When he'd doubled back, he recognized Maxwell's car parked several houses down. Approaching her house, he'd heard the man's raised voice. He'd circled around to the back. Not wanting to waste time, he'd broken a window to get in. "What the hell was going on here?"

"Harry was about to make me 'permanently his.'" She took in another deep breath. It hurt her lungs. "He thought I was Claire."

Warrick looked at her blankly. "Claire?"

She nodded. Pain shot up to the top of her head. This was going to take a while, she thought. "Claire Farrel. The first victim. Apparently, that was an accident."

"How the hell do you accidentally strangle someone?" He laughed shortly. "And all the others?"

She put it together as she went along. "I guess he thought they were Claire coming back to him. I think he probably followed each one around and when he saw someone moving in on what he thought was his 'territory,' he made sure that he wouldn't lose the girl."

Warrick looked down at the unconscious killer. "By choking her to death."

"Worked for him," she said grimly. Maxwell looked like a harmless rag doll. Just went to show how deceiving appearances could be.

It still didn't make sense to him. "But how did he get here?" They had cameras at all the exits. Were there more kills under this lunatic's belt? "Did you call Culpepper and Rodriguez?"

"I talked to Culpepper before Maxwell's little visit." Her voice was beginning to return to normal. "He has a secret tunnel."

Warrick stared at her, dumbfound. "You're kidding me."

She smiled. God, but he looked good to her. If he hadn't come when he had, right now nothing would be looking good to her. "Hey, these old buildings in the county have lots of secrets. He said he used the connection that ran through the basement. Apparently he knew he was being watched."

Warrick blew out a breath in wonder. "He's not as dumb as he looks."

She shrugged. "Survival instincts. Even the lowest creatures have them." She took a step and her legs almost gave out from beneath her. Warrick was quick to grab her before she could fall.

''Why don't you sit down?'' He nodded toward the sofa behind her.

But she shook her head. Standing up made her feel more in control, and she was still somewhat spooked over what had almost happened.

And then she looked at Warrick. He'd left in a huff and she'd thought she'd never see him again outside of the job. ''What are you doing here?''

He grinned. ''Rescuing you.''

Was he just being cute, or was there something more? ''You anticipated this?''

''No.'' He blew out a breath. The excitement had knocked his original purpose out of his head. Time to get back to business. ''I came back to apologize.'' Something he didn't do very often. Warrick shook his head, mystified. ''I don't know what the hell we're arguing about.''

''I do,'' she said. He looked at her in surprise. ''We're both scared.''

''Scared—'' About to protest that that was absurd, he thought better of it and dropped his defensive tone. After all, he'd admitted as much to himself. ''Yeah, maybe you're on to something there.''

Before she could say anything in response, someone was banging on the door. She heard Rodriguez on the other side calling to her

She smiled, relieved. It was over. ''Must be the rest of the cavalry. I'd better get that.''

He nodded. ''Good idea.'' He watched her as she went to the door. What the hell would he have done if he hadn't decided to come back tonight? If Maxwell had succeeded in killing C.J.?

He wasn't allowed to be with the thought long. The next moment her living room was filled with special agents all talking at once. Culpepper and Rodriguez had arrived at the same time as the backup team Warrick had called.

Storming in, Culpepper stopped short, looking at the floor as Maxwell began to stir and moan. "What the hell do we have here?" He turned to Rodriguez, confused. "I thought we were watching this clown."

"He outsmarted you," Warrick told him. "Maxwell knew he was being watched. C.J. said he used a tunnel that ran from the basement of his building to another one.

Rodriguez was closest to C.J. He took a closer look at her. "You look shaken up. You okay?" His eyes skimmed over her. "He didn't hurt you, did he?"

"No." She smiled as she nodded at Warrick. "Superhero here arrived just in the nick of time."

"Just in the nick of time, huh?" Culpepper peered at her throat. "Then what are those marks I see on your throat?"

Her hand went to her throat. Warrick pushed it aside, examining the damage himself. He scowled, banking down an urge to strangle Maxwell himself. "Those look pretty nasty, C.J."

She tried to sound cavalier. "I guess I'll be wearing turtleneck sweaters for a while. Good thing the weather's still cool."

They heard the sound of an ambulance approaching in the distance. "One of you ride in with him,"

Warrick said to Culpepper and Rodriguez. And then he glanced at C.J. "Wouldn't hurt for you to go to the hospital, either."

"I think Culpepper can handle—"

Warrick cut in. "As a patient."

She shook her head, raising her face up to his. Whether he liked it or not, he was her hero. And always would be, no matter what. "I'm fine just where I am."

Chapter 16

Warrick pulled his car up into C.J.'s driveway. Setting the parking brake, he turned off the engine and looked at her. They'd just spent the past two hours at the field office, filling in a groggy Alberdeen on the major salient points of recent events and explaining why their prime suspect had been wounded.

Then they had stopped at her parents' house to get the baby. Shaken, C.J. needed to hold her child in her arms, needed to feel that everything was still normal and good. She had forbidden him to say anything to her parents about this evening, only that she had a sudden urge to be with her daughter. Warrick gave her no argument.

She was still pale, Warrick thought, even when

he took the poor lighting into account. He resisted the temptation to take her into his arms and just hold her. Besides, it wasn't too prudent with the parking brake in the way. "You sure you're all right?"

"No," she admitted. It still hurt every time she took a breath. She slanted a look in his direction and smiled. It was official. He was her hero. "But I'll get there."

If she admitted that she wasn't all right, it had to be bad. The woman never listened to reason. "Damn it, why won't you let me take you to the hospital?"

She sighed before answering. It was her head that was the real problem, not her body. It was going to take her a while before she could forget how close she'd come to being victim number fifteen.

"Because nothing's broken and I don't want any sedatives. Besides, I have the best medicine in the world right there." Turning her body rather than just her head, she looked at her sleeping daughter in the car seat.

He frowned. "You don't have to tough out everything, you know."

"I know." C.J. paused, her hand on the door handle. "Would you like to come in?"

Warrick felt the ground suddenly turn to quicksand beneath his feet. "Do you want me to?"

C.J. rolled her eyes. She wasn't about to get pulled into this nebulous, gray area. "Don't start that. I don't want to play a theme and variation of the Saturday night scene in *Marty*."

Warrick stared at her, shaking his head. "You know, Jones, half the time I don't know what you're talking about."

She grinned for the first time since the blowup in her bedroom.

"Keeps the mystery alive, Warrick." And then she looked at him for a long moment. "As I recall, you said something about coming back to apologize."

It seemed like a century ago that he'd said those words. "Oh, you remember that, huh?"

"Yes." Opening the door, she got out of the car. He followed suit, rounding the hood and taking the sleeping baby out, car seat and all. C.J. fished her keys out of her pocket. "I also think I heard you tell Maxwell you loved me. Was that just to distract him?"

He watched her unlock the door. "Yes and no."

She walked inside ahead of him. Everything looked different to her. She wondered how long it would be before things got back to normal. "Which is it? You can't have it both ways."

"That's just the problem—" he shut the door behind them "—I want it both ways."

She took the baby from him. Joy stirred just a little, then went on sleeping. She resisted the temptation of taking her out of the seat and just holding her. Instead, giving in to the need to have the baby close by, she set the seat down beside the sofa and then looked at Warrick. "And you said I'm the one you don't understand? What are you talking about?"

He felt like a man on a tightrope, crossing the Grand Canyon. One misstep and it was all over. "I want you as my partner. I don't want to give that up."

She tried to read his expression and got nowhere. The man always was a hell of a poker player. "But?"

His eyes held hers as he tried to gauge how she would take this. "But I don't want to give up something else, either."

She threw up her hands. "It's like pulling teeth." C.J. planted herself directly in front of him, her hands on her hips. "What, Warrick, what don't you want to give up? Beer? Fish on Fridays? What?" she demanded. If he cared, if he loved her, why couldn't he just come out and say it? Or had it really been just a ruse? Had everything they'd just shared been an interlude?

Bit by bit, she was forcing him to shed his protective armor. To leave himself exposed. It took more courage than he'd thought. "I don't want to give you up. I don't want to give this up."

"'This'?" She shook her head. "You're going to have to get more specific than that, Warrick. I'm feeling a little dense tonight." She ran her hand along her throat. "Must have been the lack of oxygen to my brain earlier. Spell it out for me."

He didn't want to be the only one out on this limb. "You've got to give me something to work with, too, you know."

"Well…" C.J. blew out a breath, thinking. Stalling. He still hadn't said anything, committed himself to anything, not really. She didn't want to go first. "The next time a serial killer wants to kill you, I'll tell them they can't, because I love you."

That wasn't good enough. "And if a serial killer didn't want to kill me?" he pressed. "If he just wanted to wound me, would you still say you loved me?"

She turned on her heel and headed to the kitchen. In all the excitement she'd left the light on. "You ask a lot of questions."

"Answer the question, Jones." He was right behind her. "Would you still say you loved me?"

She raised her shoulders in what she hoped was a careless shrug. "Maybe."

He turned her around to face him. "C.J.—"

She caved. She knew she would. It would just have been nicer to have had him cave first. "Okay, yes, I'd still say I loved you, even if a serial killer was only threatening to wound you."

Warrick grinned at her, triumphant. "Okay, next question—"

C.J. covered her face with her hands. "Oh, God," she groaned.

He pulled her hands away from her face. A bit of sunshine was opening up within his chest around the vicinity of his heart. "*Do* you love me?"

She tried to pull away. When he wouldn't release her hands, she nodded toward the counter. "I left the coffeemaker on. I could have burned down the house."

Warrick looked at her intently. They were beyond petty distractions. "They're programmed to shut off automatically, and don't change the subject. Do you love me?"

She closed her eyes. When she opened them again, he was still looking at her. C.J. surrendered. "Yes. Yes, I love you. I'm crazy and I love you. Are you satisfied?" she demanded.

He moved his head slowly from side to side, his eyes never leaving her face, his smile never leaving his lips. "Not yet."

She groaned again. She yanked her hands away from him and turned away, afraid that he would start gloating any minute. "What is it you want, blood?"

"No, I want you to marry me."

C.J. turned around slowly. She was too young for her hearing to be going. "What?"

He saw the disbelief in her eyes and tried to interpret it.

"I know, I know," he said quickly before she could turn him down. "I've got a lousy track record, but, hey, that just means I'm due for a run of good luck. I figure it can start with you. And Joy."

She was still staring at him. "You're serious."

The quicksand was back beneath his feet. "I never joke after wrapping up a serial killer case."

"You want to marry me." She enunciated each word as if she was testing it out first with her tongue.

"Yes." He was still watching her eyes for some

kind of sign, wondering if he'd just made a first-class jackass out of himself.

She didn't believe him. He was having fun at her expense. "Why?"

What did she want from him? "Why does anyone want to get married?" He began to turn from her.

She stopped him before he could turn away. He'd started this and they were damn well going to finish it together. "I'm not asking about anyone, I'm asking about you."

"Because I love you," he shouted at her. "Because you've turned my whole world upside down and I can't seem to think unless you're somehow involved." Realizing he was shouting, he lowered his voice. The confession was painful, but maybe if it was out in the open, she'd understand. She wouldn't say no. "I always felt, because of what I saw as a kid and my own botched attempt at marriage, that I didn't have a clue how to make a relationship work. But driving home tonight, I realized that the answer isn't out there somewhere. It's in here." He tapped his chest. "And here." He touched her chest where he deemed her heart to be. Warrick looked into her eyes. "And no matter what direction my heart takes, it just keeps coming back to you."

C.J. stood looking at him for a long time, then finally uttered one word, more like a sound, actually. "Huh."

Warrick stared at her incredulously. "I've just

crawled out on a limb and spilled my guts here. I was kind of hoping for something a little more substantial than 'huh.''' Was that a smile flirting with her lips? Or just his imagination? "You still haven't answered me, you know."

She looked at him innocently. "I know."

Well, at least she hadn't turned him down. "You want time to think it over?"

C.J. inclined her head. "That would be nice."

This was going to be torture, he thought. "You going to take as long as you're taking coming up with the baby's middle name?"

And then she allowed herself a smile. A wide one. She glanced back at her daughter. Her small mouth was moving in her sleep. The baby would be waking soon. "Funny you should mention that. I've come up with one."

He looked at her uncertainly. She hadn't said anything about finding a name. "When?"

"Just now." She turned her face up to his. "And it's perfect."

"What is it?"

"Hope." The name floated between them. Her eyes crinkled. "Because that's what I'm feeling right now. Because that's what's going to be part of my life from now on."

He nodded his head. "I like it." He eyed her. With C.J. nothing was ever certain until she said it was. "So your answer's yes? I'm not taking anything for granted here."

"You'd better not. Especially not me. And, yes—" she threaded her arms around his neck and leaned her body into his "—my answer's yes."

"Good," he said just before he brought his mouth down on hers, "because I wasn't about to take no." The kiss was long and languid, melting any bones she had left. "Now let's put our daughter to bed." He grinned, stooping to pick up the car seat. "And then we'll see about putting you to bed, too."

She looked at Warrick holding Joy. Her heart had never felt this full. "Sounds like a plan to me."

*   *   *   *   *

If you enjoyed THE BABY MISSION,
you'll love the fourth book in
Marie Ferrarella's exciting miniseries:
THE MOM SQUAD
The fourth book will be available
in June 2003
from Silhouette Romance:
BEAUTY AND THE BABY
(RS#1668)
Don't miss it!

Don't miss the latest miniseries from award-winning author Marie Ferrarella:

The MOM SQUAD

Meet...

Sherry Campbell—ambitious newswoman who makes headlines when a handsome billionaire arrives to sweep her off her feet...and shepherd her new son into the world!

A BILLIONAIRE AND A BABY, SE#1528, available March 2003

Joanna Prescott—Nine months after her visit to the sperm bank, her old love rescues her from a burning house—then delivers her baby....

A BACHELOR AND A BABY, SD#1503, available April 2003

Chris "C.J." Jones—FBI agent, expectant mother and always on the case. When the baby comes, will her irresistible partner be by her side?

THE BABY MISSION, IM#1220, available May 2003

Lori O'Neill—A forbidden attraction blows down this pregnant Lamaze teacher's tough-woman facade and makes her consider the love of a lifetime!

BEAUTY AND THE BABY, SR#1668, available June 2003

The Mom Squad—these single mothers-to-be are ready for labor...and true love!

Silhouette®

Where love comes alive™

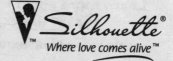

If you enjoyed what you just read,
then we've got an offer you can't resist!

Take 2 bestselling
love stories FREE!

Plus get a FREE surprise gift!

Clip this page and mail it to Silhouette Reader Service™

IN U.S.A.
3010 Walden Ave.
P.O. Box 1867
Buffalo, N.Y. 14240-1867

IN CANADA
P.O. Box 609
Fort Erie, Ontario
L2A 5X3

YES! Please send me 2 free Silhouette Intimate Moments® novels and my free surprise gift. After receiving them, if I don't wish to receive anymore, I can return the shipping statement marked cancel. If I don't cancel, I will receive 6 brand-new novels every month, before they're available in stores! In the U.S.A., bill me at the bargain price of $3.99 plus 25¢ shipping and handling per book and applicable sales tax, if any*. In Canada, bill me at the bargain price of $4.74 plus 25¢ shipping and handling per book and applicable taxes**. That's the complete price and a savings of at least 10% off the cover prices—what a great deal! I understand that accepting the 2 free books and gift places me under no obligation ever to buy any books. I can always return a shipment and cancel at any time. Even if I never buy another book from Silhouette, the 2 free books and gift are mine to keep forever.

245 SDN DNUV
345 SDN DNUW

Name	(PLEASE PRINT)	
Address	Apt.#	
City	State/Prov.	Zip/Postal Code

* Terms and prices subject to change without notice. Sales tax applicable in N.Y.
** Canadian residents will be charged applicable provincial taxes and GST.
  All orders subject to approval. Offer limited to one per household and not valid to
  current Silhouette Intimate Moments® subscribers.
  ® are registered trademarks of Harlequin Books S.A., used under license.

INMOM02   ©1998 Harlequin Enterprises Limited

Anything. Anywhere. Anytime.

The crew of this C-17 squadron will leave you breathless!

WINGMEN WARRIORS

Catherine Mann's

edge-of-your-seat series continues in June with

PRIVATE MANEUVERS

First Lieutenant Darcy Renshaw flies headfirst into a dangerous undercover mission with handsome CIA agent Max Keegan, and the waters of Guam soon engulf them in a world of secrets, lies and undeniable attraction.

Don't miss this compelling installment available in June from

Silhouette®

INTIMATE MOMENTS™

Available at your favorite retail outlet.

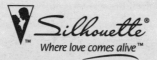
Silhouette®
Where love comes alive™

#1225 TO LOVE A THIEF—Merline Lovelace
Code Name: Danger
Before millionaire Nick Jensen headed the top-secret OMEGA
Agency, he'd led a secret life on the French Riviera, something agent
Mackenzie Blair found hard to believe—until hitmen targeted them.
As they searched for the gunmen, their professional relationship
turned personal. But would passion prevail, or would death come
under the Riviera sun?

#1226 PRIVATE MANEUVERS—Catherine Mann
Wingmen Warriors
When U.S. Air Force Lieutenant Darcy Renshaw was assigned to
fly Max Keagan to the South Pacific, she didn't know he was more
than just a sexy scientist. He was actually an undercover CIA officer
hunting his ex-partner's—and ex-lover's—killer. Intense island nights
fostered feelings Max wasn't ready to revisit, but when the killer
kidnapped Darcy, Max knew what he had to do....

#1227 LAST MAN STANDING—Wendy Rosnau
A lifetime of lies ended when Elena Tandi discovered her true
identity: daughter of a dying Mafia boss. But after years of protecting
her innocence, the last thing Lucky Massado, her father's associate,
wanted was to entangle Elena in their deadly world. For her safety, he
knew he should get her out of Chicago, but how could he walk away
from the only woman he'd ever loved?

#1228 IN TOO DEEP—Sharon Mignerey
After testifying in a high-profile murder case, Lily Jensen Reditch
moved to Alaska and met Quinn Morrison, her new employer. They
shared a whirlwind romance, and she finally felt loved, safe—but not
for long. The man Lily helped imprison had put a price on her head,
and someone had come to collect—someone Lily would never
suspect....

#1229 IN THE ARMS OF A STRANGER—Kristin Robinette
Police chief Luke Sutherlin, Jr., knew better than to fall for a prime
suspect, but when she was as sexy as Dana Langston, that was no
easy task. The loving way she held the unknown baby in her arms
made it hard for him to believe *she* could have murdered the child's
mother. However, Luke knew that he had to uncover the truth—before
he lost his heart forever.

#1230 THE LAW AND LADY JUSTICE—Ana Leigh
Why were defendants from Judge Jessica Kirkland's courtroom
turning up dead? Detective Doug McGuire was determined to
find out. Sparks flew as the rule-breaking cop and the by-the-book
judge hunted for an obsessed serial killer. But soon the *hunters*
became the *hunted*, and if Doug didn't reach Jessica in time, the
verdict would be death.

SIMCNM0503